Magic

The Endonshan Chronicles, Volume 4

Cy Bishop

Published by Cy Bishop, 2017.

MAGIC

First edition. December 15, 2017.

Copyright © 2017 Cy Bishop.

ISBN: 979-8230465317

Written by Cy Bishop.

With special thanks to:

God, my patient family, Google,

and Jessica Dodson for the fantastic cover

'The Endonshan Chronicles' follows key
events in the historical timeline
of the planet Endonsha.
Each story is told from the perspective of
individuals best positioned to give the
clearest understanding of the event.
Book 1: DragonBond
Book 2: Sanaraheim
Book 3: Power
Book 4: Magic
Book 5: Invasion
Book 6: Traitors
Book 7: Feral

334 years before The Division

Chapter 1

Ari pretended to be fixated on the snarls in her father's net as she listened to the little footsteps sneaking up behind her. Hiding a smirk, she tilted her head and leaned closer as if scrutinizing a knot, waited for just the right moment, then spun and threw the net over the 'prowler.'

"Hey!" Tashan protested and shoved at the elaborately knotted ropes. She pouted at her older cousin. "How'd you know I was there?"

Ari rolled her eyes. "Just because all the palace guards are near deaf doesn't mean everyone is, Tash." She pulled the net off and resumed her work. "What are you doing out here?"

"I want to train."

"You know your mam doesn't want you out here." Or out of the palace at all, but especially not all the way here at the northern docks. The shallower fishing river, compared to the deep southern trade river, meant fewer people; expansive swamps north of the river meant fewer threats; and fewer people and fewer threats meant fewer guards. Great for Ari and her parents, not so great for keeping a curious young princess safe.

Tash shrugged and bounced up onto a dock post next to Ari, looking like she belonged there with her grubby 'street wear' clothes and a wide leather cuff on her wrist to hide the shimmering tattoo that marked her as royalty. "I wouldn't have to come all the way out here if you still lived in the palace."

Ari bit her tongue so fast, she nearly drew blood. She pretended to be focused on her work. The eight-year-old princess had never understood why her favorite playmate left the palace, and Ari wasn't going to be the one to tell her. It never helped to speak ill of someone else's parents, and besides, Ari was more than happy to pretend none of it had ever happened. Tash didn't always make that easy.

Tash looked down at the steady river beneath them as it flowed west around the city of Innsbrooke, where it ultimately poured into a lake surrounding the aforementioned palace's island. "I'm sorry. I know you don't like it when I ask about that."

Ari shook her head. "You really should go back. I don't want you to get in trouble." Or for Queen Savini to find out Tash was still visiting. The queen had insisted from the beginning that Ari, being so much older, was a poor influence. That opinion had only gotten worse as Ari progressed further into her teenage years. If only she knew it was more often the other way around.

"I won't. They won't notice I'm missing until dinner. That gives us lots of time for training." Tash scooted closer to the edge of the post, waiting expectantly.

"I'm not good at your type of training. Neither are you, for that matter." Ari tugged another snarl free.

"That's why we need practice."

Ari rolled her eyes again. "Tash," she said in her best chiding tone.

Tash hopped down and tugged at Ari's long sleeve. "Come on, Ri-Ri," she said, over-emphasizing the flip on the *r*'s. "Please?"

Ari prodded the last knot. She shouldn't agree. Tash would get in trouble if they were caught, and Ari would get into even more trouble. And their 'training' never went well.

But her cousin was right that they needed the practice. The magic tutor that came once a week to help train the kids in the swampy area had been displeased with Ari's consistent lack of improvement. He kept saying that she had so much energy, it shouldn't be hard for her. He told the others in the class that she was an example of what sort of bad magic use happens when people don't bother trying to control it. Ari's fingers tightened on the knot at the memory of her humiliation, accidentally yanking it tighter.

"There are lots of people in the streets today," Tash tried again. "And I know a warehouse that's empty."

Ari set the net down and eyed her cousin. "Lots?" More people meant less chances the guards would notice the two of them in the crowd. Especially since Ari hadn't reached her 'growing point,' as her mam called it, and was barely half a head taller than the much younger princess.

"Lots and lots." Tash's monolid eyes gleamed with excitement. "We'll blend right in. No one will notice us."

Ari stayed quiet a moment longer as if thinking, but she and Tash both already knew what her answer would be. "Fine, we'll train."

Tash squealed and jumped up and down, clapping her hands. "Let's go!" She was already halfway down the dock toward the bridge into the city by the time Ari got to her feet.

Ari followed her cousin into the city, both of them first hiding amongst groups of people crossing the bridge and then sliding through alleys and behind crates to avoid being seen. She finally caught up when Tash stopped a few blocks from the south docks.

Tash grinned and pointed to a dilapidated warehouse. "Isn't it great?"

Ari frowned at it. "We're going to burn the whole thing down."

"No, we won't." Tash elbowed her cousin. "Because we're going to make sure our fire doesn't get too big. We didn't set anything on fire last time, remember?"

No, they'd nearly been spotted by guards instead. Ari peered for any signs of patrol, but there were no signs of people around at all. Most of the workers must be down at the docks, not unusual for this time of day.

"Besides," Tash continued, "this warehouse is supposed to be torn down soon, anyway. I heard the guards talking about it. That's why I chose this one."

"That doesn't make things much better," Ari muttered.

Tash pulled her toward the warehouse, but Ari resisted, taking another look. She had to be sure there weren't any guards around. The warehouse stood near the ledge of the wall that bordered the walkway down to the docks. A cautious peek proved that most of the activity was at the far end of the docks. There was hardly anybody walking near the sparkling waters far beneath them.

Tash sighed impatiently. "You're so paranoid."

"You want to get in trouble?"

"We won't. Now come on!"

Easy for the princess to say. She might get sent to bed with no dessert, or get a nanny parked on top of her until she found a way to evade yet another babysitter. But Ari knew what it meant to be in trouble with the queen as someone outside her favor. It was still too recent that her family had been locked up—sequestered, as the queen put it—in seclusion in the palace. It was only Tashan's determination to keep sneaking in to play with Ari that earned them their freedom in the form of banishment to the northern swamps. The best thing that happened to them—Ari would rather live in the swamps for the rest of her life than set foot in the palace again.

The warehouse was, as Tash promised, empty. No crates to set on fire, no piles of straw to singe. Even the rafters were lofted high above them. Ari studied the space, trying to compare it to the size of fireballs she'd seen her cousin set off. Or the ones she'd accidentally set off herself. She cringed internally and clamped down her focus. She wouldn't let it get away from her this time. She wouldn't.

"Making fire is the first step to real magic," Tash recited, taking on the airs of a tutor. "It's the easiest to master, and once you master it, you can master any of the other types of magic."

"Easiest to master, pfft." Ari shook her head.

"The key is control," Tash continued, reciting the words they'd both heard over and over. "You—"

"Do you really have to go through the speech every time?"

Tash frowned at her. "Control is the part we both have trouble with, so listen up."

Ari hid a laugh at how much her little cousin looked like the tutor with her pinched expression.

"As I was saying," Tash said loudly before going back into her speech, "you have to release enough energy to create the flame, but only that much. If you release too much energy, you'll have too much fire. So keep the rest of your energy under control. If you can't control it, you can't do magic."

Ari cringed with each sentence. That was the part she couldn't do, no matter how hard she tried. "Are you sure this is enough space?"

Tash laughed. "Come on, Ri-Ri, don't be a scaredy-braybun." She turned to the wide space ahead of them and held her hands out. "I'll go first."

In the space of an eyeblink, a massive fireball exploded in the center of the room. Searing heat sent both girls tumbling backwards into the wall. The fire swirled and vanished.

Ari coughed, covering her nose and mouth with her sleeve, but the heat was already fading to nothing. "Tash?"

"Ouch." The younger girl rubbed at the back of her head where she'd hit the wall.

Ari kept her eyes down for a minute. "That was bigger than last time."

"I tried to make it smaller," Tash protested. "I tried to use control."

"At least nothing caught fire." Ari glanced over some scorch marks on the rafters indicating how close they'd come. "We should leave."

"No! I can do it, honest." Tash scrambled back to her feet.

"Tash—" She reached for her cousin's arm.

The fire reappeared, smaller this time but still way too big. Ari threw an arm in front of her face against the blaze.

"Ri-Ri!" Tash shrieked.

Ari lowered her arm to see the singed rafters now ablaze. Panic shot through her. "No! No, no, no! Put it out!"

Tash screwed her face up and held her hands out toward the fire. It was just a matter of drawing back energy to put a fire out, the tutor said. Just a matter of control...

"Come on!" Ari shouted.

"I'm trying!" Tash clenched her teeth and eyes shut, hands shaking with effort. "Help me!"

A lance of terror shot through Ari. She would only make things worse. She tried to control it, tried to keep her energy back, but it always burst out too much, even worse than Tash's.

"Help!" Tash cried again.

Ari clenched her fists and focused on the fire. She tried to keep her energy under tight control, to hold it firmly so it wouldn't feed the flames. She had to draw energy back, not let it out. Draw energy back... Draw it back... She inwardly strained, struggled against the energy that wanted to come out.

Nothing was happening. The flames reached the roof. A chunk of burning wood broke free and crashed to the ground.

Ari grabbed Tash. "Go!" She dragged her cousin out of the building.

Outside, Tash broke free. "We have to put it out!"

Voices shouted; people down at the docks had spotted the fire above. "We have to go! Someone else will put it out!"

"No, this was our fault, and we have to fix it!" Tash screwed up her face again, hands extended toward the flames. They grew.

"Stop it!" Ari cried. "You're making it worse!"

"Then help me!"

Ari spun to the building, focusing in a panic.

The entire roof exploded with flame.

She screamed, stumbling backwards just as a massive column of water rose up from the river and crashed over the roof.

Tash grabbed her hand and pulled her down one side street after another, finally ducking them both behind crates as the voices and pounding footsteps faded in the distance. The younger girl panted. "I don't think anyone saw us."

"Saw us? How about the part where we almost burned down an entire building?" Ari clung to her sides, shame and inward anger tearing her up. She'd tried to help and made it worse. As always. She pulled her knees to her chest and buried her face, closing her eyes against the coming tears.

"It's okay," Tash soothed, lightly stroking Ari's wild red curls. "It's all right now. One of the people had magic and made water come from the river to put the fire out. Did you see it?"

Ari nodded, face still buried.

"So everything's fine now."

"We destroyed a warehouse."

"Yeah, but it was going to be torn down anyway, remember?"

Ari shook her head. "That doesn't make it okay. No more training."

"Okay. We can stop for today."

Ari hadn't meant just for the day, but she didn't have the heart to say so. She leaned back against the wall, letting her hands fall in her lap. "I hope that person gets some sort of reward for stopping the fire."

Tash shrugged, toying with the strap on her wrist cuff. "Maybe. I don't think a lot of people get rewards they should when they do good things." She wrinkled her nose. "I don't know why."

"Well, you can change that when you become queen."

Tash made an even bigger face.

Ari eyed her cousin. "What?"

Tash was quiet for a moment, her focus still on the strap. "Can I tell you a secret?"

"You know you can."

"I don't want to be queen."

"Yeah?" Ari straightened and raised an eyebrow out of curiosity, not surprise. The idea of not wanting to be a ruler was nothing strange to her. Her mam had never been interested in the power Queen Savini was convinced Mam wanted to steal. "Why not?"

"I don't know. It just sounds really big. I don't know if I'd do a good job taking care of that many people."

"I think you'd do a great job. There's a lot of good things you could do—rewarding people for good work is just the beginning."

"My mam does a lot of good things. She could just keep being queen."

Ari started speaking and barely caught herself in time to temper her words. "I think... I think you could do a lot more good things. Even better things than your mam. You'll be an amazing queen."

Tash made a face again. "Queen Tashan. Ugh. I don't like how that sounds."

"Really?"

Tash shrugged. "I don't know. 'Princess Tashan' sounds okay. 'Queen' just sounds weird."

Ari smiled and ruffled her cousin's hair. "When you're in charge, you can call yourself whatever you want." She adjusted her skirt, feeling better. It had been long enough; no one was coming after them. "I think my mam and da want to see the procession this year. Will you wave to us if I tell you where we'll be standing?"

Tash's nose wrinkled again. "We're not going to be in the procession this time."

"You aren't?" Every year, the guards gathered for an official procession through the city to the docks on the lake. The royal family came across on a grand boat, and they rode behind the procession down the main road in a beautiful carriage pulled by a team of veelish, the lanky animals with their long, soft fur just as majestic as the carriage. After a speech from the queen at the east gate of the city, the procession returned the royal family to the palace. Ari had never heard of the royal family skipping the event.

"It's the lunar new year for the second moon, and it's the seventh year," Tash explained. "The Tulvans are all gone on their pilgrimage to the temple."

Ari had forgotten about that, unsurprising since she'd been fairly young the last time it happened, and her family had already been secluded from the rest of the palace at that point. The powerful fighters were the ones who always monitored the palace and protected the royal family until the procession of guards reached the docks. "Is the procession not happening this year?"

"No, Mam says it's important," Tash said. "But the guards are worried we won't be safe with everyone on procession and the Tulvans gone, so they're going to have one of the High Lords give the speech, and we're..." She clapped a hand over her mouth. "It's supposed to be a secret."

"They're going to hide you somewhere else for the day," Ari said.

Tash's eyes went wide. "How did you know?"

Ari couldn't help but chuckle. "Just a guess." She stood and helped her cousin up. "I guess I won't see you then."

Tash grinned. "You will. I'll come and play as soon as we get back."

"Hey!" Both girls jumped and turned to see a guard coming their way. "You kids shouldn't be playing around here. This is a dangerous area."

Startled, Ari looked around and realized Tash's winding route might have brought them far west of the destroyed warehouse, but they were still only a couple blocks from the docks. And in a particularly slummy area, at that. She cringed away from the guard, unsure what to say.

"It's okay," Tash said without a blink of hesitation. "We're not causing any trouble."

The guard frowned down at them. "Where are your parents?"

Ari bit her lip, glancing the opposite direction for an escape route. She hated trying to talk to guards, whether it was here in the city or back in the palace when she was younger. The guards, the High Lords, the king and queen—her tongue tied itself in knots before a single word could escape.

"I said, we're not causing any trouble," Tash repeated, planting her hands on her hips. "So leave us alone."

"Tash!" The exclamation burst from Ari's mouth before she could stop it. She caught her cousin's arm. "Sorry, sir. We're leaving." She kept her head down away from the guard as she turned to scoot away.

"Hold on. I'm not done talking to you," the guard barked, his growing displeasure obvious.

Ari cringed again as she felt her feet obey in spite of her desire not to.

"You're not being very polite," Tash scowled at the guard. "Guards are supposed to be nice and help people."

Ari's grip tightened. Tash never filtered herself, speaking whatever came to her mind. "We're sorry, sir. Our parents aren't far. Please let us go." Ari wasn't sure if she was speaking loudly enough to be heard. She could barely hear it herself over her angry heartbeat. Guards never left her alone. It had been a mistake to come in the city at all.

"Maybe you two need to learn a lesson in respecting authority," the guard snapped, striding toward them. "Let's have a chat with your parents." He caught each of them by the arm.

"Hey, let go!" Tash squirmed.

Ari shrank, her tongue returning to knots. They could show their matching tattoos and be released in seconds, but then they'd have an armed escort to the palace. Tash would be in trouble and sent to her room, and that would leave Ari standing alone in front of the queen with nothing to say in her defense.

"Now, which way are your parents? Or should I just take you to the outpost?" The guard eyed the road to the docks as if he preferred the second option.

"I said, let us go!" Tash shoved the guard with her free hand.

He scowled and yanked on Tash's arm, shaking her hard and drawing a cry of pain. "That's enough out of you!"

The anger pulsing beneath Ari's learned submission exploded into her limbs. "Don't hurt her!" she screamed, her fist slamming into the guard's jaw. He reeled backwards. Tash grabbed Ari's hand and bolted. Angry words and curses chased after them for several blocks before finally fading to silence.

As soon as Ari felt it was safe, she slowed, pulling Tash to a stop beside her. "You better go back home now."

"I can't believe you punched him!" Tash grinned.

"I'm serious, Tash. We could get in real trouble. You need to go to your home, and I need to go to mine, and we need to avoid the guards in the city for a while."

Tash heaved an over-dramatized sigh. "Okay, okay. I don't know why he was being such a grump. He was nice when he was working at the Meeting Hall."

Ari shot her cousin a look. "You recognized him? How come he didn't recognize you?"

"He's part of the city guard that helps at the Meeting Hall sometimes during celebrations. He's been there twice—no, three times. His name is Ivn, I'm pretty sure. I don't know why he didn't recognize me. Though he was always near the doors, so maybe he just didn't see me as much."

"How do you remember all those details about everyone?" Ari asked, shaking her head.

"I don't know." Tashan shrugged. "Can we play again tomorrow?"

Ari heard footsteps. "Sure, we'll do that, but you have to go home. Right now, got it?"

Tash nodded, then slipped down a crossway and vanished from sight. The tiny Kadrian girl had always been good at that—better than Ari—which was how she got out of the palace unnoticed so often. And how she had continued visiting them in the palace back when the queen locked up Ari's family.

A bitter taste hit Ari's tongue, and she forced her thoughts away from the past. She checked to make sure the other way was clear, then hurried off before the footsteps got too close. As much as she hated the constant reminder of where she'd come from, she loved her cousin. Tash would be a good queen. A great queen. And the sooner she became queen, the better.

As long as she didn't let her impulsiveness get her into trouble first.

Chapter 2

Tashan waited behind a barrel as a group of men walked past, each carrying large crates and talking with big gestures, their voices louder than the noise that always surrounded the south river docks. She tried to listen in, but couldn't understand much of what they were saying—something about 'pretty raisas' and showing off to them. She knew 'raisa' was the polite word Elves used for women, like how they said 'tabe' for men, but that didn't help her understand any better.

The men never glanced her way, and before long they were far enough away that she could slide out from behind the barrel and continue to the docks, making her way toward one of the bridges. Once she was across the river, it would be easy enough to get to the secret tunnel that went under the lake, going from a cave hidden in the forest south of the river to the palace. It was supposed to be for the royal family to escape if bad guys reached the palace. Tashan thought her use of it, getting in and out of the palace undetected, was way more fun.

Another group of workers emerged from a nearby ship, unloading cargo, and Tashan ducked down a side alley. The sounds of people hollering to each other and crates thumping together got a little quieter as she moved toward the next street running parallel to the docks. It wouldn't hurt to stay on that street for a while before trying to cross the bridge. That was always the hardest part, since guards closely watched the way in and out of the city. The wide, long bridge didn't offer a lot of places to hide, either.

But she always found a way. Usually she hid herself with a group of people crossing; other times she relied on her grubby clothes to disguise her enough to pass unnoticed. Once she had even climbed along the underside of the bridge, weaving through the beams that supported it, when she'd realized the guard on duty was one she knew well from the palace. Yelek. He always looked the other way when she wandered into the kitchen before dinner to find an extra sweet-glazed hardroll.

A raised voice grabbed her attention, less because it was loud and more because it was saying her mam's name. The rest of the sentence was muddled by his voice dipping and rising at odd points. "Savini... have to... at all!"

Another voice shushed the first, and more voices joined into a quieter conversation. It was coming from a building just ahead. Tashan slid against the wall and moved slowly until she had a better view of it.

The building didn't stand out from any of the others except for maybe a few more boards covering the windows. Da said this area had unsavory people, which didn't make sense because 'unsavory' means they taste bad. But Tashan understood what he meant to say, that there were bad people near the docks. Tashan glanced around, feeling a little shiver at the reminder that this wasn't a safe place for a princess to wander. She probably should get closer to the docks again, where there would be more guards in case she needed help. But first, she wanted to hear what these people were saying about her mam.

It was easy enough to get through the clutter outside the front of the building and underneath the window near the door. The boards made it so the people inside couldn't see her, but she couldn't see them, either. She craned her neck at different angles, trying to get a peek, but couldn't see anything except a bit of light on the ceiling. She decided not to bother, sinking low to remain unseen behind the damaged crates and discarded barrels. Better to stay hidden and listen than to peer in the window and risk being seen.

"Try to focus, gentlemen," a sharp voice said, different from the loud one earlier. This one made her think of some of the teachers that came to work with her in the palace, particularly one magic tutor who always sounded like he'd rather be working with someone else. "The building is ours for the remainder of the month. The guards only pay attention to the cargo coming in and out. They'll think nothing of our activities. We'll be able to get everything in place without them knowing a thing."

Tashan's heart sped up, and she leaned in excitedly to hear more. It sounded like there was some wicked plot in the works. Maybe she could find out what it was and tell the guards before the bad guys could do anything.

"This is ideal as our staging area," the sharp voice continued. "In the few days left, we'll make sure everyone and everything is in place."

"Yeah, we got it," a pinched voice replied impatiently. "And what do we do until then? Sit here and play cards with the wastiks crawling all over us?"

The sharp voice was the loud one this time. "Mind your tone. It's only a matter of days before the procession of the guards. Everything must be perfect by then. We're only going to get this one chance, and we better get it right."

Tashan leaned even closer to the wall, listening hard. Whatever these bad guys were going to do, it would be during the procession. But that didn't make sense—who would want to try to do something bad on the day all the guards were out in the city with everyone watching? That meant there would be lots of witnesses. It seemed like a silly choice.

"Keep an ear open for any changes." Sharp-Voice sounded like he was coming to the end of his speech. "Notify us immediately of any deviation, no matter how minor it may seem. And remember, it's vital we get the whole royal family. It won't work if we just kill the queen and king. We have to get the kid, too."

Tashan's insides turned cold, then very, very hot. Kill them? These guys wanted to kill her and her parents? Her legs fought to carry her forward so she could throw open the doors and make a fireball right in the middle of the room.

But she resisted. Ari always said she was making decisions too fast and should think before acting. These guys wanted to kill her. Maybe going closer to them would be a bad idea. What would Ari tell her to do? Get away from bad people. Tashan scrambled to her feet to run back to the docks. She would find a guard, and the guards would come and—

A massive hand clamped on her shoulder. She squawked, but before she could do anything, the guy holding her had already thrown the door into the building open and shoved her in ahead of him. She stumbled over her feet and would have fallen, but the painful grip the giant Kadrian man had on her shoulder kept her up, almost dangling instead of standing.

A whole bunch of people looked up from the table they stood around, making frowns and scowls at her. A Nim man, taller than even the other Nims at the table but just as wiry, had the biggest scowl of them all. "What's this?"

It was the man with the sharp voice, the one who said they were going to kill her and her parents. Rage twisted Tashan's face. "You can't kill the queen and king! They're important, and they're good people, and I won't let you!"

The leader laughed. Tashan ignored him, already gathering her energy for the biggest fireball ever. She would show them!

The hand on her shoulder tightened. It was as if all the gathered energy flickered away like the last few seconds of a firework. Her eyes drooped, her eyelids suddenly heavy. "Wha…" She felt large hands catch her as she tumbled into sleep.

TASHAN FELT SOMETHING hard and scratchy under her. Her back ached. She smelled hay and something less than clean. Where had she fallen asleep, the stable? Why hadn't any of the guards woken her up to go back inside? She pushed through the last bits of sleep and sat up.

An older Nim woman, bronzed skin lined with gentle wrinkles, jumped to her side and pushed her back down. "There, there, now, hush and lie still."

Confusion took over Tashan's mind. Who was this? Not one of the guards or any of the attendants. The old woman kept talking in a soothing voice with lots of shushing, her high, sloped forehead stretching and wrinkling in time with the rise and fall of her eyebrows. Tashan looked past the woman, trying to solve her confusion. The ceiling was lower than it should be. Three stone walls, rough and in worse condition than anything at the palace. The last wall was made of metal bars.

Tashan sat up again, fear pounding its way through her veins. This wasn't home. Where was she?

"Hush, hush," the woman repeated, trying to ease Tashan down once more, but Tashan was too scared to relax.

"Where am I? Who are you?" She tried to sound brave, but her voice shook.

"You're okay. I'll keep you safe." The woman pulled her close into a smothering hug, looked back at the metal bars, then leaned her head down so her mouth was beside Tashan's ear. "I know who you are." The Nim's voice was barely audible, even from so close. "You mustn't let anyone know you're the princess. If they find out, they'll kill you."

Terror replaced the confusion. She'd overheard people talking about killing her mam and da, and now those same people had captured her. The fear turned back into anger. "They can't do this! They can't! We have to stop them!" She tried to push free from the woman, ready to charge for the bars and blast anyone she could see.

The woman's grip was iron strong. "Hush, hush, child. I'll keep you safe." She rocked back and forth, humming.

Tashan tried to break free again and failed. Without warning, hot tears of frustration filled her eyes and slipped down her cheeks. She felt the woman's arms shift, sliding just enough so the woman could stroke her hair. Tashan clung to her and sobbed.

She wasn't sure how long it was before her sobs faded into hiccups. The woman slowly relaxed her grip, still humming, and Tashan sat back with a sniffle. All the fight had gone out of her.

"My name's Pahmi," the woman said, handing over a soft cloth for Tashan to clean her face with.

Tashan took the cloth and dried away the last of the tears, shifting her weight and trying to get comfortable. The 'bed' under her was nothing but some burlap covering a mass of straw. She wasn't sure what to say now. Pahmi already knew who she was. "Where are we?"

"In a small castle south of Innsbrooke, about half a day's walk from the city," Pahmi said. She pushed silvery hair behind her ears with one hand while the other hand took the cloth and wiped a spot Tashan had missed. "One of the High Lords fancies himself a proper king of his own little kingdom and has created as much here."

Tashan frowned. "Which one?"

"I don't know. I didn't even know this castle was here until I made the mistake of wandering too close to its grounds while searching for some morrowroot. They took me prisoner for trespassing."

"Just for trespassing?"

"I think they don't want people to know this is here." Pahmi settled down on another bed like Tashan's. "I've been here nearly three months, as best as I can tell with no window to gauge the time."

Tashan looked over the blank walls. "Are they going to keep us here forever?"

"I believe they're waiting for the High Lord to inspect his prisoners and decide their fates." Pahmi's lips twitched upward. "It lets him keep the illusion of being in control of his world."

It took Tashan a moment to figure out what the older woman was saying. This High Lord wanted to think of himself as the ruler here, so he would deal with prisoners himself, the way a ruler would. Her mind moved back to a different puzzle. "Morrowroot?"

"It's a medicinal plant that eases pain. I'm an herbalist. Do you know what that is?"

Tashan nodded. There was an herbalist who visited the palace, though not very often. The palace healer took good care of them, so there wasn't any need for someone who heals using plants and ointments rather than magic. But Mam said it was important to show support and respect for all professions, and so she would summon the herbalist once a month for a special tea that helped her relax.

"I hadn't found any in my usual areas, so I went on further to keep looking. The next thing I knew, several men were dragging me down here." Pahmi gestured around at the cold walls and metal bars, her sloped brow crinkling new lines into all the wrinkles.

Tashan scowled. "That's awful. We have to get out of here and get the guards. They'll come here and take the place apart!"

"I'm sure they would, but there's no way out."

"I'll make a way!" Tashan jumped to her feet, focused on the bars, and unleashed her energy. A massive fireball burst to life. Pahmi shrieked, and people in other cells hollered, too. Tashan fought to bring the fire back into a controlled size, but heard Pahmi shout again. Looking over her shoulder, she saw flames dancing on the older woman's shirt sleeve.

"Oh no!" Tashan cut off the energy. The fireball vanished, but the fire had fixed itself on Pahmi's shirt. Tashan focused on drawing the energy away from the flames. This one was much smaller than the one in the warehouse, and she was able to draw it away and extinguish the flames.

Pahmi clutched her arm, taking deep breaths to steady herself.

Tashan dropped to her knees next to the older woman. "I'm sorry! I'm really, really sorry. I didn't mean to hurt you."

After a few more breaths, Pahmi shook her head. "You only got my shirt, not me. I'm all right. Shaken, but unharmed."

Tashan pushed back the tears that wanted to fall. "I won't do it again, I promise."

"That would be best." Pahmi examined the new, charred hole in her sleeve. Her arm underneath had turned red.

"What's going on here?" a woman demanded, scowling at them from outside the cell.

"Nothing," Pahmi said, resting her arm as if there was nothing wrong.

The guard scowled, but someone at the end of the hall of cells said something to her, and she snorted and walked away.

Tashan looked down at her hands, unsure what to say. Her fireball had done nothing to the bars, nothing to help them. She'd only hurt instead.

Pahmi was the one to break the silence, keeping her voice low so no one else could hear. "We should decide on a name for you."

"A name?" Tashan matched the Nim's volume.

"You can't use your own," Pahmi reminded her. "You need something to give them when they ask."

"They're going to come here?" Tashan looked at the hallway. She wouldn't try to burn the bars again, like she promised, but she could burn the bad guys. "When?"

"The guards bring meals through and check on us from time to time, but their leader—the High Lord's second in command—always comes and checks on things when new people are brought down. He'll probably come before too much longer today."

Tashan looked up at the windowless walls. "I can't see the sun. How do you know when it's today and when it's tomorrow?"

Pahmi smiled and adjusted Tashan's hair. "The guards follow a schedule. We still have a few hours left before tonight, and after that will be tomorrow. Now, for a name. We should choose something that isn't too different from your real name, in case one of us makes a mistake."

"Like Tasha? Ooh! My cousin calls me Tash. Will that work?"

The older woman considered it. "That's probably too close to your real name. What about Toshi?"

"Toh-shee," Tashan said slowly. "It's different. I think I like it."

"Toshi it is, then." Pahmi held out a hand in greeting. "Delighted to meet you, Toshi."

Tashan couldn't help but giggle.

Thumping feet drew her attention back to the hallway outside their cell. She started toward the bars to investigate, but Pahmi caught her wrist and pulled her back with a little head shake. Tashan gave the bars one more look, then reluctantly sat down. She would have to wait until whoever it was got close enough to sneak a peek at. She hated waiting.

Fortunately, the wait wasn't very long. A group of men appeared, Sharp-Voice and the giant Kadrian walking at the front of the group just behind a Kadrian man with an oddly angled face, as if something had been bent when he was formed. He walked the same way Mam walked when she was about to address her subjects.

"Here," Sharp-Voice said, stabbing a finger in Tashan's direction. "She was listening in outside the window. Henin caught her before she could sneak off and tell anyone."

The giant, apparently Henin, bobbed his head in agreement with Sharp-Voice's report.

Angle-Man inspected Tashan from head to toe. His voice came out smooth and hard all at once, like a newly forged blade. "You were speaking loudly enough for any random urchin to overhear?"

Sharp-Voice's face turned bright red. "Of course not! We—" He cleared his throat. "That is, we weren't being loud. She just happened to decide to spy on us."

As they yammered, Tashan focused on collecting her energy. She had to be careful this time, extra careful about how much she let out. She didn't want to accidentally hurt Pahmi or the other prisoners, but the fire had to be big enough to get all the bad guys. She took a deep breath, then let it out.

A flash of light appeared, but disappeared just as quickly with a hand wave from Henin. He snorted and rolled his eyes at her. "Thought you might try something again. Mind your manners, or I'll put you back to sleep."

Tashan glared at his mocking grin. She'd figured out the sleepy thing he'd done—he had to be a healer, which wasn't very common, and he'd used his healing energy to make her body relax so much she fell asleep. She'd thought that meant he wouldn't have any way to stop a fireball. She'd never heard of a healer who could also use the more common types of magic.

Angle-Man raised an eyebrow toward Henin. "And that was?"

"The kid has some decent power in her. Given the right circumstances and encouragement, she could be a strong asset."

"But a risk until then."

"Nah. She's got no control over what she does. She's just as likely to burn herself up as anyone else."

Tashan's ears turned hot. "That's not true!"

The smaller Kadrian crouched to her level, tilting his head in a way that made the angle look even more pronounced. "Curious. Clean this one up, and I think she'd look rather similar to Kenara's beloved little princess. And with magic in her, too." He shook his head. "If I didn't know the princess was safe and snug in the palace and didn't run around the streets dressed like a dock rat, I'd say we could have royalty on our hands."

Pahmi's grip tightened. Tashan looked down at the floor, afraid she might say or do something that would give her away. Her heart thudded loudly enough she was sure they would hear it and know.

Sharp-Voice scratched his chin, looking Tashan over. "I don't see it. The princess has a rounder face."

"Similar, I said. Not identical." Angle-Man straightened and brushed himself off before leveling a glare at Henin. "If she burns this place down, it's on your head."

"She won't. She's not that stupid."

One of the men toward the back of the group shifted from one foot to the other, as if he wanted to take a step further away from Tashan but didn't want the others to know that. "Easy for you to say, magic user. You can protect yourself against that sort of thing."

Henin rolled his eyes again. "So keep some water on hand."

"Keep talking like that, and I'll decide she's too much of a risk to keep around," Angle-Man snapped. He paused, looking back at Tashan once more. "Though I imagine there could come a point where a doppleganger of the princess could be quite useful. For now, she's of no use to our plans, but contingencies never hurt. What's your name?"

Tashan was so distracted by her fear that it took a moment to realize he was speaking to her. She shot a look at Pahmi, unsure what to do and afraid the man would figure out she was the princess. Now it felt like 'Toshi' sounded too much like 'Tashan.' Could she still use it?

"Well?" Angle-Man demanded. "I'm not a patient man, little girl. Answer me."

Pahmi shook her head no with a tiny motion so the guards wouldn't see.

Tashan thought frantically to come up with something else, something she wouldn't forget—or forget to answer to. Ari's face filled her mind. "Ree. My name is Ree." She pronounced it with a flat 'r' sound instead of the flip in her cousin's name, but it was close enough that it would be easy to remember.

"Well, Ree, here's the deal. You don't start any fires, and I don't kill you. Got it?"

Tashan felt a shiver, and she wasn't sure if she was more scared or angry at the moment. Pahmi squeezed her arm, gentle but firm. "Yes," she said quietly toward the floor.

"Good." The group of men moved on, still talking.

Tashan strained to hear, hoping for any clues that might help her escape and stop them. She managed to pick up 'palace' and 'secret passage' before they were too far away for her to hear anything more. She felt cold inside. Secret passage? Did these men know about the hidden tunnel out of the palace? Were they going to try to sneak into the palace using the passage?

But that made no sense. The hiding room the tunnel led to was barricaded and could only be opened from inside, on the palace end of the tunnel. And these men were too big to use her way in and out, through the tiny drain spaces built into the walls. They must have meant something else.

"You did well," Pahmi said quietly, settling against the back wall. "Good thinking on the name, too—Ree."

"I could have done more." Tashan plopped against the left-side wall with a pout. "The big guy keeps making my magic stop."

"That's for the best. If you had attacked them, they likely would have killed you for it." Pahmi gave her a stern look, like how Mam looked whenever she discovered Tashan had snuck out of the palace again. "You need to be more careful. Don't give them any reason to think it's too dangerous to keep you locked up here."

Tashan poked at some of the straw that had wandered loose from the bedding. "I'm sorry."

The older Nim unfolded her long legs and scooted over to sit beside Tashan and wrap an arm around her. "I just want to keep you safe." Pahmi's wrinkled face turned toward the hallway for a moment, then leaned closer. "Now, let's figure out how we're going to get you out of here."

The shame and sadness vanished into a rush of excitement. "Really? You think we can escape?"

Pahmi smiled and pushed hair out of Tashan's face. "If there's a way, we'll find it. I promise."

Chapter 3

By the time the guards brought lunch the next day, Tashan wanted to climb the ceiling and claw her way through the stones. She and Pahmi had talked late into the night, discussing the guard schedules and the layout of the castle—the little part Pahmi had seen, at least. The morning alternated between talking through ideas for how to escape and attempts at gaining better control over her magic.

Neither had resulted in any real progress. Every idea Tashan came up with for how to escape was either something that had already been tried or 'not feasible,' as Pahmi kept saying. And every time she sat in the corner, facing the stones so she couldn't accidentally hurt anyone and doing her best to make her energy create exactly what she wanted it to create, she ended up with singed hair, blackened stones in front of her, and no success in finding control.

"Come. Eat," Pahmi said, her voice gentle and steady.

"I don't want to eat!" Tashan kicked at the straw mattress beside her. "I want to get—" Pahmi gave her a sharp look, and Tashan coughed on her next words. She folded her arms. She couldn't even shout properly in here, for fear of giving away too much of what they were trying to do.

Pahmi handed her some stale bread dipped in something greasy and nasty smelling. If it wasn't for the fact that it was all the food they would get for hours, Tashan would have thrown it against the wall, or better yet, at the next guard to pass by. Tashan scowled as she bit into the chewy mass. Her stomach rumbled. If she was home, she would be sitting down to a full meal with sweet-glazed hardrolls for dessert. The sadness felt a sword that dug into her, and she pulled her knees to her chest, hugging them tight with her free arm. She just wanted to go home.

The Nim lightly stroked Tashan's hair for a minute, finishing up her own food before speaking. "I could teach you some things, if you like. I don't know much about magic, but I know how to calm the body and strengthen focus."

Focus. That was one of the many things her magic tutors said she was missing. Tashan nodded. It wasn't like anything else they were doing was getting them any closer to escaping.

They finished eating, then sat facing each other. "Close your eyes and focus on your breathing," Pahmi instructed. "Slow breath in, and slow breath out." She closed her own eyes and repeated the last line, demonstrating the breaths as she did so.

Tashan closed her eyes and copied the older woman's breathing. "Okay, now what?"

Pahmi chuckled. "You have to do more than just one breath, child. Focus on how the breaths feel, one after another."

"Okay." Tashan's nose crinkled, but she closed her eyes again and took another breath. Then another. And another. Bored, she peeked at the hallway. Maybe talking about 'not feasible' ideas and practicing on her own would be more helpful than this, after all. Pahmi was still talking, repeating the 'slow breath in, slow breath out' line. Tashan fiddled with a loose string on her shirt. How was this supposed to help her focus?

A clatter of noise came from the end of the hallway. Tashan straightened, craning her neck in case she could see anything without being rude to Pahmi. Nothing. She sighed and returned her attention forward.

Pahmi's eyes were open, and she was looking down at Tashan with a knowing smile. "Go and see, if you must."

Tashan scrambled to her feet and raced to the bars, pushing her face against them hard so she could see as much of the hallway as possible. Guards grunted and said not-nice words, and someone was yelling a stream of threats and insults. It sounded like a real fight. A rescuer, maybe? Like in the stories, where a brave person swoops in and saves the day. Tashan's heart sped up in eagerness as she strained to see.

A guard reeled backwards from what must have been a strong hit, slamming against a cell on the opposite side of the hallway. He snarled under his breath and rushed back in, the fight now close enough that he didn't completely leave Tashan's view. Closer—she could see legs violently kicking, managing to knock the same guard back again.

Finally, the fight moved into sight. Three other guards clung to an Elf with black hair and skin the color of fresh mud. His eyes, solid color like all Elf eyes, were black and seemed to have lightning shooting across them as he continued shouting at the guards. He couldn't have been more than a teen—it was hard to tell with shortened Elf height, but he might not have been much older than Ari—and yet the adult guards had trouble keeping control over him as he thrashed and flailed.

Tashan clutched the bars of her cell. "You can do it! Fight!"

The Elf kicked off the wall, forcing the knot of people to stagger sideways into the opposite wall, one guard all but getting pinned between it and the angry fighter. The others added their limbs to the flailing mess, trying to catch and still the Elf.

Footsteps from the opposite direction were barely audible over the commotion. "You weaklings can't keep hold of one little Elf child?" a guard said with a mocking sneer.

"Shut up and help us," the guard squished into the wall grunted.

"No! Let him go!" Tashan demanded.

The new guard smacked a hand against the bars just beside her face, making her jump backwards, then he joined in the fight. The five guards working together were able to push and pull and drag until the Elf was in the cell beside Tashan and Pahmi's, the wall blocking him from Tashan's view entirely. The metal door clanged shut as the Elf continued shouting, the bars rattling as if he was pounding against them. The guards said some stuff she couldn't hear, and then went back to their posts.

The ruckus continued in the other cell for a few minutes before gradually quieting down. Tashan pressed as close to the wall as she could get and wrapped one arm between the bars to wave through the bars of his cell. "Hey. Are you okay?"

No one answered for a minute, and Tashan was worried he'd been injured. But then he spoke, his voice strangely calm. "Swell. Best workout I've had in years."

"I think you could have beat them if that other guard hadn't come along."

The boy laughed. "Thanks, kid. So, what are the odds you have an escape tunnel already built over there?"

Tashan blinked, unsure what to make of the question, then realized he was joking. "Sorry. No escape tunnel."

"Guess I'll have to make my own then." His arm came into view, extending from his cell and waving her direction. "I'm Korent. And you?"

"I'm T—I'm Ree. It's nice to meet you." The mannerly words came automatically and sounded weird in this setting.

Korent's hand waved upward, the fingers puckering together as if making a pointed beak, and the 'beak' bowed low. "A pleasure to meet you, raisa. Now if you'll excuse me, I need to work on our escape."

"Escape?" Her heart sped up again with a new burst of hope. She remembered to lower her voice with a cringe, but no guards seemed to have noticed. She stage-whispered, "You know a way out of here?"

"Nope." The hand withdrew. "But figuring it out's half the fun."

"Perhaps we can work together," Pahmi said, startling Tashan. She hadn't heard the older woman come up behind her. She realized she'd been so distracted and upset by the whole situation that she was forgetting her best skills, her ability to sneak around unnoticed and tell when people were coming.

The hand reemerged with a second polite bow. "Raisa-ro. You shouldn't have to put yourself in danger for this. I'll find a way to get us all out."

Pahmi's knowing smile returned. "Of course. I simply thought we could provide advice and suggestions." Tashan frowned at Pahmi—they could do a lot more than advise, they could help—but the older woman waved for her to stay quiet.

Korent seemed to consider that for a moment, his hand withdrawing once more. "You've been here for some time?"

"I have, though Ree's new." Pahmi sat down near the wall. "My name's Pahmi, and I can tell you everything you need to know about the guards and their schedules."

Tashan listened for a few minutes before she was bored of all the information she'd already heard. She wandered back to the sleeping pallet and sat on it, poking at the straw. Lumpy stuff. She sighed and pulled out a few pieces, twisting them between her fingers before tossing them on the floor. Maybe she should go back to practicing her magic. She scooped up the discarded straw and went to the opposite corner from Pahmi. Lifting the straw in front of her face, she focused on only letting out enough energy to ignite them and nothing more.

Instead, it all came out in a burst, like always, and the flames blazed with such ferocity that she squeaked and scrambled backwards. She rubbed at the coating of soot on her arms. She wasn't getting better—she was getting worse.

"What happened?" Korent demanded. "Are you hurt?"

She pushed away from the blackened corner. "I'm fine." She didn't want to talk any further than that.

Pahmi took over for her. "She's practicing to gain better control of her magic."

"Magic?" Curiosity trickled through his tone. "You can do magic?"

"She's learning," Pahmi said, her tone similar to how Mam spoke when she was trying not to say something bad about someone who had done a bad job.

Korent was quiet for a couple minutes. "Does that mean you can make fire, Ree?"

"I make too much of it," she grumbled, pulling her knees to her chest and burying her face against them.

"Perfect!"

She looked up. "What?"

As he spoke, she could hear his grin. "That's perfect. Now, if only we had a way to—"

Footsteps came from down the hall, quiet but approaching. "Shh!" Tashan hissed. "They're coming."

"I don't hear anything," Korent said, a frown in his voice.

"Shh!" she repeated.

About a minute later, the incomers arrived with the angle-faced leader, the sharp-voiced man from the docks, and Henin at the front. They stopped in front of Korent's cell this time. "This?" Angle-Man said with a snort. "This little pup is what gave you all that trouble?"

"I'd be happy to demonstrate," Korent offered. "Open the door."

Tashan pressed against the bars for a better view as a guard scowled, a fresh bruise swelling one eye shut. "This 'little pup' is probably from one of them villages what trains them in fighting since before they can hardly walk. I'd like to see *you* try to pin him down—" Angle-Man gave the guard a dark look, and the guard quickly added, "—sir."

Angle-Man seemed to consider the guard's face a moment longer before addressing Korent. "Quite the fighter, then. You could earn your freedom and a hefty purse if you put those skills to use for us. You'd like to be part of something powerful, wouldn't you?"

"Sure," Korent said.

"What?" Tashan pressed her face harder against the bars. He couldn't! But then she realized how overly bright his tone had sounded.

"Sure, I'll help," Korent continued. "Open the door."

"I see." Angle-Man rolled his eyes, but chuckled. "Quite the spirit on that one. We may have use for him eventually. Keep an extra eye on him for now."

Tashan frowned. It would be hard to make their escape plans if the guards were watching Korent too closely. The group of men continued on their way, and she stuck out her tongue at them as they passed. Most of them ignored her, but Angle-Man paused. He looked her over, then his gaze flicked to the back corner of the cell, the one darkened with soot from her practice. She realized how much soot was probably on her face and looked down, embarrassed.

"Not getting far, are we?" Angle-Man said with a smirk.

"I can keep her asleep," Henin offered.

Tashan's fingers tightened into fists, but she knew there was nothing she could do to prevent it if he did.

"Don't bother. She's more likely to crisp herself and the old woman than to do any real harm to any of us."

"No, I won't!" Tashan snapped, glaring.

Angle-Man laughed and continued walking, the others following after him. A guard leaned against the end of a wall separating cells on the other side of the hallway, watching Korent's cell.

Tashan looked back at Pahmi. Now what would they do?

Pahmi shook her head slightly, pretending to be focused on adjusting the straw in one of the mattresses.

Turning back, Tashan made a face at the guard. He, however, was looking toward the end of the hallway, where the voices of the leader's group were rapidly fading. As soon as the voices were gone, the guard snorted and pushed off the wall. He smacked a hand against the bars on Korent's cell and wandered down the hall.

"They never hold a post for long," Pahmi explained in a whisper. "They stay at the ends of the hallways so they can hear when their leaders are coming, and then they run back into place."

"Hey," Korent said, his fingers waving through the bars at them. "How'd you know they were coming?"

Tashan shrugged before remembering he wouldn't be able to see that. "I've had a lot of practice listening for people coming. I can tell where people are around me when I remember to listen."

"All the better."

The last thing he'd said before the guards and bad guys interrupted was that it was perfect she made too much fire. "What do you mean?" She scooted closer to the wall between their cells and whispered. "Do you have an escape plan?"

He matched her tone. "I think so."

"Well? What is it?"

He hesitated. "I wish we had a way to talk more privately. Anyone overhearing could put the plan at risk."

Tashan sighed. If she had mastered fire, she could have learned how to move rocks around by now. "I know, but there isn't."

"There might be," Pahmi supplied. "Back this way." She led Tashan to the rear of the cell and knelt beside some of the stones on the side wall, her lanky legs folding awkwardly under her. She poked at some crumbly mortar between two of the slabs. "I noticed a hole in the mortar when I was first placed in here, and I've been working at it since. I've made it to a pinpoint hole on the other side, but couldn't get much further."

"Where?" Korent's muffled voice was almost impossible to hear through the wall.

Pahmi took a long piece of straw and poked it through the hole. "Right there. See it?"

There was no answer, then the straw pulled free from Pahmi's hand and disappeared through the hole. Then some light appeared, growing stronger as Korent pried away the mortar on his side. He leaned close and peered through at them. "Hi."

"Hi," Tashan grinned, waving.

"Can you hear me clearly?" he asked. She nodded. "Good," he said, his voice taking on a firmer edge, like someone who expected to be listened to. "You're going to make a fireball inside my cell. I'll pretend to be really hurt, and they'll come to open my cell door. Once it's open, I'll take them by surprise, get the keys, free everyone else, and we'll all get out of here."

"Sounds great!" Tashan wiggled, eager to get started, but paused. "You said it would help that I can hear people coming. How?"

"For when we make our way out. You can help us avoid running into too many of these guys until we've made it to safety."

"It's a courageous plan," Pahmi said gently, "but Ree's magic use can be... dangerous. I don't want you to be injured for real. Unintentionally, of course."

Tashan pulled her knees to her chest again, her face growing uncomfortably warm.

"The more dangerous it is, the better they'll believe it," Korent said, undaunted. "You can aim it toward the front of the cell, right, Ree?"

"I think so." It would be hard without being able to see, but she could try.

"So I'll stay close to the back, low and flat so I'm less likely to get burned. It'll work."

Pahmi still seemed concerned, but moved on. "And what happens if too many come for you to face? Perhaps we should add a few more details to increase our likelihood of success."

"There won't be too many. I won't let them get the better of me again." Pahmi looked like she was trying to figure out how to say something without being mean about it, but Korent spoke again before she did. "Well... maybe a couple more options wouldn't hurt. What did you have in mind, raisa-ro?"

"It won't be much longer before they bring us the day's end meal, and after that, the night guards come for duty. They get bored quickly and don't pay much attention. If we wait for a little while after the day guards have left, we'll have the best chances of facing the fewest guards at their most unaware."

"Good thinking," Korent said. "We'll wait and do it then."

"I also think we might be better off if we give them a reason to open our cell as well," Pahmi said.

"Why?"

She hesitated again before proceeding carefully. "Should it happen that you are overwhelmed, as unlikely as that may be, if the guards have already opened our cell, we will still have a chance for escape." The older woman's gaze flitted to Tashan, and her voice dropped even lower. "It's very important that we get Ree out of here. Do you understand?"

Tashan could see just enough to tell he had a confused look on his face, but he nodded, saying, "Very well, raisa-ro. I'll see to your wishes." He paused. "How? Should she make a fireball in your cell, too?"

Pahmi shuddered. "No, it wouldn't help. They wouldn't open the door with her still in here and able to make another attack."

Tashan looked around the cell, and her eyes stopped at her mattress. "But what if I wasn't here?"

"If you weren't here, then all our problems would be solved because we could just follow you through your escape route," Korent said. He paused. "You said you didn't have an escape tunnel, right?"

Tashan made a face at the teasing tone, hoping he could see her expression through the hole. "No, I mean, what if they *thought* I wasn't here?"

Pahmi looked over her shoulder, and her face lit with understanding. "I see. You are small enough to pass, I think."

"Pass? Someone want to let me in on the plan?" Korent asked.

"I'll hide under the mattress," Tashan grinned. "It's perfect."

"And they won't notice the distinctively Ree-shaped lump under the burlap?"

"No," Pahmi said. "Because we're going to pull out most of the straw and arrange the rest around her. She's small, so her body won't stick up much higher than the rest of the straw. It won't look too much different than it does now."

"Hey, that's cool. I like it! Hmm... and all the straw we pull out? Are we going to eat it? Because I'm not really that hungry."

"You'll put it near the front of your cell, and she'll burn it with the fireball she makes," Pahmi said.

"Straw doesn't burn in a flash. They'll see the burning pile of straw and know something's up."

Pahmi looked down at her charred sleeve. "With her fire, that won't be an issue."

Tashan looked down in shame. "I'm sorry."

"Don't be," the Nim said with a gentle smile. "I believe this plan may work. Your fire will be our way out."

A bubble of warmth spread through Tashan's chest, and she smiled back. "I think it'll work, too."

"Excellent." Korent wiggled a finger through the hole. "Shake on it."

Tashan giggled and pressed her finger against his, and they both moved their fingers up and down in a mock-solemn shake. Pahmi looked amused as she did the same. Tashan stuck a finger toward Pahmi, and with a laugh, Pahmi 'shook' her finger, too.

After their meager dinners were delivered, Tashan sat by the bars, listening and watching the hallway as much as she could. The stale rolls tossed in at them didn't require any plates or utensils, so there was nothing for the guards to collect, which meant no guards walking past the cells anytime soon. Pahmi and Korent worked studiously removing straw from Tashan's mattress and passing it through the hole, now made wider with a bit more digging at the crusty mortar.

Tashan listened as the new guards arrived for night duty and reported this to the others. The day guards talked and joked for a little while, but finally their footsteps and voices faded away. Only the night guards were left. Tashan scooted back over and saw the mattress was nearly empty now. "Where are you piling the straw?"

"Just inside the bars, where they won't be able to see from the end of the hall." Korent gestured toward the front of his cell.

Tashan pressed her face as tightly against the wall as she could, moving her head up and down until she caught a glimpse of a few dry shafts poking upward at the top of the pile. "Okay."

Pahmi lifted the burlap and had Tashan lie down, then arranged straw around her before replacing the burlap. She adjusted a few places before lifting the rough cloth again, looking satisfied. "You'll need to see the place you want to start the fire, right?"

Tashan sat up carefully so she didn't disturb the ring of straw around her. "As close as I can, yeah."

"Then you'll have to move quickly. Start the fire, then get straight to your position here, and I'll cover you up before they get here and see you."

"Okay." Tashan's heart skittered in a cross between excitement and fear. What if it didn't work? Or if she hurt Korent for reals instead of for pretends? What if they didn't fool the guards?

Pahmi took her hand and squeezed it. "Ready?"

She put on the bravest face she could and nodded.

"Are we set?" Korent asked through the hole.

"Ready when you are," Tashan said, hoping her voice didn't tremble as much as it felt like it did.

Korent met her eyes through the hole and winked. "You're going to be awesome." Then he disappeared from view, probably getting into position away from the fire. "Okay," his voice came, faint through the distance, "I'm ready."

Tashan returned to the flat position against the wall and found the pile again. Even though she could only see the top, it would be enough for her to get the fire on target. She hoped. Taking a deep breath, she gathered her energy together and aimed it for the pile, trying to focus on making it big enough to attract attention but not big enough to hurt Korent or whoever was in the cell opposite him.

The front of Korent's cell exploded in fire. Tashan leapt for her 'mattress' and dropped flat just before hearing panicked shouts. One of the voices sounded like Korent. She sat up. Had she hurt him?

Pahmi pushed her back down and swiftly tucked the burlap in place. "She's gone!" the older woman shrieked. "She disappeared!"

"Help! Fire!" Korent wailed, followed by indistinguishable cries of pain.

The sound clenched at Tashan's heart until she remembered that the plan was for him to pretend to be hurt. She forced herself to take deep breaths. That was all it was. He was just pretending.

Clattering footsteps announced the guards were already there, arriving in the span of seconds. "He's burned!" a deep voice boomed. "Get the key!"

"The kid is gone," a slightly higher voice came from just outside their cell. "How is the kid gone?"

Tashan closed her eyes and held her breath. A moving mattress would give them away for sure.

"Where did she go, old woman?" yet another voice demanded as the sound of keys twisting in a lock came from Korent's cell.

"I don't know!" Pahmi sounded almost hysterical. "She was here, and then that fire, and now she's gone!"

"Call for the medic," someone from the hallway said.

"Bring those keys over here," the higher voice demanded.

"Let's see the burns, boy," the deeper voice said from inside Korent's cell.

"Aaagh! It hurts!" Korent wailed.

The keys jangled, then twisted in the lock as the guards in the hall continued to shout over each other. Tashan curled her fingers into fists, trying to keep from letting out her held breath in a burst.

"Get out of the way, old bag," a man snapped as he entered. "Lek, hold her in the hallway while I check the cell."

Pahmi's stuttering footsteps exited the cell.

Tashan felt her chest instinctively jerk in protest against the lack of air. She clenched her teeth. At any moment, Korent would act. Unless he really was hurt and wasn't pretending. She wanted to throw off the burlap and rush to the hole to check on him, but somehow managed to hold back the impulse. *Please, Korent, be okay and attack them like we planned*, she thought desperately.

A roar came from the next cell, a mighty battle cry.

"What the—oof!" Something big smashed against the wall. The voices came even louder and more frantic now—and aimed toward Korent's cell.

In her relief, Tashan lost control over her held breath and sucked in a new one. Was she spotted, or had the guards been too distracted by Korent to notice? Should she jump up and run out now, or wait to see if a better moment came?

The fight sounded big, and it sounded like it wasn't going well for the guards. Tashan held herself back as long as she could, but finally she couldn't take it anymore. Sliding her arm as carefully as possible, she pushed the burlap up just a tiny bit, just enough to see.

A guard stumbled back against the opposite cell, blood all over his face. The guard in Tashan's cell was already leaving, heading for Korent's cell. It was working!

"Get the hag locked up!" the man snarled at the guard holding Pahmi. "We'll find the brat later!"

The other guard nodded and shoved Pahmi into the cell. Tashan's chest tightened. They had to get out before the guards could lock the cell again. But how?

Pahmi apparently had the same thought, because as soon as the guard turned her focus onto the lock, the older woman spun and kicked the door squarely in the center, sending it smashing into the guard's face. "Run! Now!"

Chapter 4

Tashan scrambled to her feet, throwing the burlap aside and racing for the door. Pahmi had already left the cell, shoulder braced against the door to keep it open. Tashan jumped over the older woman's feet and ducked under the wide swing of a guard trying to grab at her. She shrieked as she barely avoided another grabbing hand coming her way.

"Go!" Pahmi shouted above the chaos. "Run!"

Most of the guards were around Korent's cell, so Tashan bolted the opposite direction. The other prisoners pressed against their bars, screaming at her as she passed. Most sounded like they were cheering her on, but it was hard to tell. All her focus was on the end of the hallway, where a stairway curved upward with no guards in sight. Loud footsteps clumped after her, too far behind. If she could make it up the stairs, she could find a corner to hide in before the guards chasing her could spot her.

A hand from a nearby cell swung at her, fingers extended to grab her arm. She shrieked again, dodging. She had to stumble to keep from losing her balance, but managed to keep herself upright and racing forward. The stairs were just ahead. Her heart thundered. She was going to make it.

"Hey!" A guard appeared on the stairwell, startled by the sight of a little girl charging at him.

"Grab her!" yelled a second guard behind him.

Tashan yelped and backpedaled, almost falling to the floor. She looked around frantically. A stairwell with guards coming at her. A hallway with two guards chasing her. And nowhere else.

She bolted back toward her pursuers. Only two there, so she had a better chance of getting past them. The guards slowed and braced themselves to catch her. She waited for the last possible moment, then ducked into a ball. One of the guards yelled a not-nice word as Tashan rolled right between his legs.

Tashan planted her feet at the end of her roll and let the momentum carry her upright. Now she just had to get past the mass outside Korent's cell.

A hand clamped on her elbow, yanking her backwards so hard she fell to the floor. The other guard smirked, her eyes cold and hard. "Nice try, kid."

"Let go!" Tashan shouted, trying to break free, but the guard's grip was too tight.

The first guard caught Tashan's other arm as the new guards from the stairway rushed past, joining the fight. "Come on," he grunted. The two of them dragged Tashan back toward her cell.

Tashan felt like she couldn't breathe as she kicked without making any difference. Pahmi was already back in the cell. Korent hadn't made it out of his cell, and with the new guards that had come, there were too many for him to fight through.

They'd failed.

The guards reached the cell, ready to throw her in, but then a loud voice broke through all the noise. "What is going on here?" Angle-Man's voice.

Grunts and thuds continued from inside Korent's cell. The guards outside parted as Angle-Man stormed to the door of the cell. He cast a sneer of disdain at the guards and slammed the cell door shut, knocking a couple of guards further inside. He held out a hand, and the key was handed over without a word. The sounds of fighting quieted as the key turned into the lock, sealing everyone in. Within moments, the cell was completely silent.

"Would someone like to explain?" His voice was calm, but his face was anything but.

Several guards spoke at once. "There was a fire—" "I heard shouting—" "The boy was hurt—"

"You!" Angle-Man barked, silencing the others with a sharp jab toward one of the guards inside the cell. "Explain."

The guard held onto the bars, seeming unsure whether he was going to make it back out or not. "Uh, sir, there was a fireball, and the boy was hurt. Or he said he was hurt. And the old woman was screaming that the girl was gone."

"This girl?" Angle-Man eyed Tashan.

The guard bobbed his head, making his heavy beard shake. "She wasn't inside the cell. I looked, and I swear she wasn't there."

Angle-Man snorted. "Until she came running out of it, I wager."

"What are your orders, sir?" the guard asked, sounding like he hoped the question would make Angle-Man happy with him. "Should we kill the boy?"

"No!" Tashan shouted, lunging forward, but the guards yanked her back, tightening their grips until her arms throbbed.

Angle-Man narrowed his eyes at her, then at the cell. "Bring the girl here."

The two guards pulled Tashan forward until she stood beside Angle-Man. She stole a peek into Korent's cell, and her insides dropped. As beat-up as the guards looked, he looked even worse. He sat on his mattress, slumped forward. The guards around him looked ready to hit him if he tried to move.

"Boy," Angle-Man said sharply.

It took a moment, but Korent finally looked up, one eye nearly swollen shut.

Angle-Man met Korent's gaze for a moment, then turned and backhanded Tashan across the face hard enough to almost knock her off her feet. She gasped, too stunned to do anything more than that. Little lights danced around her suddenly watery eyes.

Pahmi cried in alarm. "She's just a child! Leave her alone!"

Korent shouted at the same time, "Monster! Don't you dare lay a hand on her again! You hear me? Don't you dare!"

He had barely finished speaking when Angle-Man yanked Tashan's hair to turn her face upward, and he slapped her again. She heard nothing but a dull roar, and her legs gave out. She sagged against the hands gripping her. Korent and Pahmi were still shouting, she could dimly tell. Then the grip on her hair came again, forcing her face upward once more.

"Stop!" Korent shouted, suddenly sounding desperate. "Please. I'll do whatever you want. Just don't hit her again."

Angle-Man kept his grip on her hair for a long moment, then released it. Her head dropped forward, heavy and dull, her face feeling numb and on fire all at the same time. The man stepped back, brushing his hands off. "This is what happens when you pretend to be some fierce warrior, boy. Do you understand?"

"Yes. Yes, I understand."

"Then stay put while my guards leave."

The lock clicked once more, and a dozen shuffling feet made their way out of the cell. Tashan felt awareness returning but couldn't convince her legs to hold her. Her body shook with sobs as tears streamed down her burning cheeks.

The last guard slammed the door shut behind her and turned the key, locking Korent inside once more. Angle-Man patted Tashan's head, then waved dismissively. The guards shoved her inside her cell, the bars ringing as the door banged back into place right behind her. She stumbled forward; her legs still didn't want to hold her. Pahmi caught her and gathered her into warm, comforting arms, hurrying back to sit against the wall at the rear of the cell as if the distance would prevent the guards from touching them again.

"This one's trouble," the deep-voiced guard said. His voice was slurred; he'd probably been hurt in the fight. "Why don't we just kill him and be done with it?"

"I abhor a mess." Angle-Man turned and walked away. "We'll report to the High King when he returns. He can decide the boy's fate. Until then, quit falling for pathetic escape attempts." He paused. "The new recruits should be here by morning. We'll station some down here, since you lot are apparently incompetent to mind the prisoners on your own."

Pahmi hummed and stroked Tashan's hair as the guards went back to their posts. Tashan clung to the older woman, her mind and body still trying to get through the shock. No one had ever hit her before.

"I'm sorry, Ree," Korent said, his voice quiet. "I'm so, so sorry. I never thought you'd get hurt."

"It wasn't your fault," Pahmi corrected. "It was a good plan. They just had more guards here than we thought."

"But if I had fought better, we could have been out of here before more guards came. I screwed it up."

Tashan's voice finally returned to her. "You fought really well. I'm sorry you got hurt, too." It came out thin and wobbly, but loud enough for him to hear. "Pahmi's right. It wasn't your fault." She tried to take a deep breath. It caught on a hiccup. "We can try to figure out something else—"

"No." Korent's voice was sharp. Then it softened. "I'll try to think up some way to get the two of you out of here, but not me. I won't give him a reason to hurt you again."

Tashan sniffled. "But I don't want to leave you here."

"That's enough for now," Pahmi said, firm and gentle at the same time. "We'll all feel better, and think more clearly, after some rest." Her voice dropped quieter. "Korent, are you hurt badly?"

He grunted in a way that almost sounded like he was trying to laugh. "No worse than the end of a training session. These guards hit like children." He hesitated. "And Ree?"

"I'm okay," Tashan said, though her voice still shook.

Pahmi hugged Tashan closer. "She'll be fine after some rest."

Something about the warm arms holding her close was comforting. Like when Mam picked her up and cuddled her tight. A fresh burst of tears came, and she turned her face into Pahmi's shoulder. She wanted to be back home, cuddled in Mam's arms again. She wanted to be out of this awful place with these awful people. She wanted to be safe.

The older woman resumed humming and stroking her hair. "I know. It's going to be okay," she murmured from time to time. The tears finally slowed into hiccupy gasps, and sleep took over from there.

Tashan awoke to rumbling footsteps, the sound of many people tromping down the stairs at one end of the hallway. She sat up and found herself on Pahmi's mattress. The Nim sat near the bars of the cell, watching down the hallway. "What is it?" Tashan whispered, crawling closer.

"Their new recruits, it seems." Pahmi looked over, then licked a thumb and used it to wipe something off Tashan's cheek. "Feeling any better?"

Tashan sat next to the older woman, maybe closer to her side than she would have usually sat by someone. "I guess so." Her face no longer hurt, but her insides ached and twisted around. She didn't know if it was even possible to get away, and now she wasn't sure she was brave enough to try. Angle-Man hurt her because Korent tried to escape. Who would he hurt if Tashan tried to escape—Pahmi? Korent? She didn't want to see anyone get hurt because of her.

Pahmi wrapped an arm around her and pulled her a little closer without saying a word. It was like the Nim understood already.

Tashan sighed and leaned her head against Pahmi's shoulder, partly for a better look at the hallway and partly because it felt good to lean into the woman's comfort. "Can you see them yet?" It sounded like they were getting closer, and Tashan could almost make out what they were saying.

"Not yet."

It didn't take long before the group of men and women filled the hallway, Angle-Man leading them. His talk was boring, only giving directions on how to watch the prisoners and not saying anything that might be useful to know.

"I expect you all to keep alert and watching. Don't think that just because they're locked up, they can't cause any trouble," Angle-Man continued, shooting a glare toward Korent's cell. "Listen and watch at all times."

A tall Elf with thick arms spoke loudly. "Why bother to keep them around? It'd be easier to just kill them all."

The man beside him, a thin-faced Nim with eerily sunken eyes shook his head. "Not all. Some can have their uses. But for the rest, it does seem to be a waste of resources." His dark eyes locked on Pahmi and Tashan. "Especially on those who aren't even fit to break and keep as slaves."

Angle-Man narrowed his eyes at the Elf, then addressed the Nim. "What's your name?"

"Rishi."

"I like how you think, Rishi. But it's the High King's decision to make, so we keep the prisoners held until he returns."

"How long is that gonna take?" the Elf asked, making a face toward the cells. "I signed up to fight, not to babysit. You said this would be done in a couple days, right? So he could come here today and—"

"Two days remain before we act," Angle-Man cut in sharply. "The High King has a tight deadline and is quite occupied making sure everything is in order. He can't risk taking a trip out here when we're so close to completion. Nothing can go wrong—especially not a problem with the prisoners because of lazy guards unwilling to do what they're paid to do." He gave the Elf a meaningful look. "It will likely be a week, perhaps longer, before he is able to step away from his work and come here. He would be most displeased if anything fell out of order in his absence."

The Elf snorted. "Yeah, we get it."

"We will," Rishi spoke over him. "If babysitting is what you're paying us to do, then that's what we'll do. I can't see how it would be difficult. You have solid stone walls and iron bars. The only way I could see any trouble is if someone was stupid enough to open a cell door."

Angle-Man actually smiled at that, a rather disconcerting look on his odd face. "You're going to go far here, Rishi." His gaze flicked to the Elf. "Others, not so much. Let's get you equipped and assigned to your duties."

Tashan leaned forward so she could watch as the group filed out. Angle-Man cast a glance her way. She scowled at him, letting anger cover up her fear. He smirked and walked away.

As soon as the footsteps indicated the group was far enough away, Tashan crossed to the other side of the cell and sat next to the hole in the mortar. "Korent? Are you awake?"

"Nope."

She made a face at the hole. "Yes, you are. You just said something."

"Really? Are you sure?"

"Come on." She drew out the last word. "We gotta start working on our new plan." Between the three of them, they had to be able to come up with something that would get them all out without being caught. They just had to.

There was a stirring of movement, and Korent sat next to the hole. His face was even more swollen and discolored today, and his joking tone disappeared. "No. I told you, I'm not going to let them hurt you because of me again. I won't put you in danger."

"But you aren't. I'm putting myself in danger. I want to get out." She had to bite her tongue as more words tried to come. She *had* to get out. She had to warn her parents.

"It's a tabe's job to protect the raisas. I can't let you put yourself at risk."

She scowled. "Try to stop me." With that, she flounced back to the mattress and plopped down on it, folding her arms with a cross glare she hoped he could see through the hole.

He sighed. "Ree..."

"I don't want to talk to you unless you're going to help."

"All right." And he said nothing more.

Tashan scowled again, hurt that he wasn't willing to help. She looked at Pahmi. "He's too scared to help, so we have to make a plan ourselves."

Pahmi leaned her head back against the wall and spoke too quietly for anyone outside their cell to hear. "Most of the High Lords would recognize you on sight, wouldn't they?"

Tashan nodded.

"The man said we have about a week before this High Lord comes, so we have to find a way to get you out before then."

"But he said they have two days before their plan. I have to get out before then so I can warn my mam and da."

Pahmi sighed. "Two days, with extra guards watching us, and no one else helping us?" She looked down, and Tashan could tell the older woman didn't think it was possible. But Pahmi straightened and gave Tashan a small smile. "We'll keep thinking. I'm sure we can come up with something."

Tashan leaned back, putting on her best thinking face. "Could we trick a guard into coming in here with the keys?"

"Probably not. Their leader made it fairly clear they are expected to keep the doors closed."

"What about getting one close enough with the keys that we could reach through the bars and get them?"

Pahmi shook her head. "Only one holds the keys, and that guard is required to stay near the stairs."

"But if they thought there was an emergency?"

"I don't think it would work." Pahmi gave her a kind, sad look. "After what happened last night, I believe they'll be extra careful about opening those doors. I don't believe we'll be able to fool them again."

Tashan sighed and bumped her head back against the stone wall. "We got enough mortar out to see into Korent's cell. Can we get more out and break through the wall?"

"We're underground on this level, and the other two walls only lead to more cells."

"We could dig out, though."

Pahmi looked down at her hands and didn't answer for a long time. When she did speak, she sounded like she didn't want to say anything. "I don't think it would work. It would take too long, and with extra guards, they would see what we were doing before we got far."

Tashan stomped at the floor, which was awkward with her seated position. "If I was good at magic, we could just open it all up at once. We could even get everyone out."

Pahmi didn't say anything. She just pulled Tashan closer.

No new ideas came, no matter how hard Tashan thought. She finally wandered back to her own newly thinned mattress and curled up on it, facing the wall. She knew why Pahmi didn't want to say anything. The older woman didn't want to make her think it was hopeless.

But it was hopeless. There was no way out. These horrible people were going to kill her parents, then her, and there was nothing she could do to stop it. Fresh tears slipped across her nose and dripped onto the mattress.

She was still crying when she heard footsteps in the hallway. She half-heartedly looked over her shoulder. The cramps in her belly told her that it was probably a guard bringing those nasty rolls. It was never enough to quite fill her up, and it didn't seem worth bothering with today. She put her head back down.

The steps paused at each cell, followed by soft thudding sounds of the rolls being tossed in at the prisoners. Her mind automatically tracked where the guard was. The cell on the other side of Korent's... Korent's cell... their cell...

Oddly, the guard paused longer than he had at the other cells. Curiosity beat the sadness, and she took a peek. It was the creepy-eyed Nim that said they should just be killed. Rishi. He was staring at her with those dark eyes as he dug in his bag for the rolls. He pitched one in her direction, then tossed a few toward Pahmi. He stared at Tashan a moment longer, making her want to squirm and cringe away. To her relief, he finally continued on to the next cell.

She turned back to her side, glad he was gone. Why had he stared like that? Did he recognize her? Her chest tightened with fear.

Pahmi crouched closer to her. "Did you recognize that man?"

Tashan shook her head no.

"Might he have recognized you?"

Tashan shrugged. The fear was already disappearing into the sadness. They were going to kill her anyway; what difference did it make if it was now or later?

Pahmi lightly rubbed Tashan's shoulder. "It's going to be okay. We'll figure something out."

Tashan shrugged again.

Pahmi sighed and picked up the roll behind Tashan, placing it in front of her. "Please at least try to eat." She kissed Tashan's temple before moving back to her own mattress.

New tears stung through the sadness. It felt so much like something Mam would do. She closed her eyes and hugged her legs close.

Her belly's complaints grew until she finally couldn't ignore them anymore, and she reluctantly picked up the roll. One edge was broken, like it had been cut into. She poked at the spot, letting her finger slip inside the roll and feel the overly rough bread. Blech.

Something else caught her attention as her finger pressed in deeper. Something with a hard-ish edge. Frowning, she sat up and pulled the roll apart. A folded piece of paper landed in her lap.

Her heart sped up inside of her. A note? Who would give her a note? Why? She almost felt afraid to let in the hope that it was someone who could help them escape. Her fingers felt too clumsy as she hastily unfolded the paper.

I'm from the Innsbrooke guard. I've been tracking these people and finally managed to infiltrate them. I know who you are, but I'm guessing they don't. They wouldn't keep you down here with all the other prisoners if they did. There isn't much I can do without exposing both of us, but I will do whatever I can to get you out of here safely. I will come tonight at midnight. Pretend to be asleep.

Tashan's breath caught, and she read the note twice more. "Pahmi!" Her voice came out a squeak.

Pahmi was at her side in an instance. "What's wrong?"

Tashan showed her the note without a word, and the older woman read it over, her eyes brightening with each line. She clutched Tashan's hands. "This is it! This is how we'll get you out!"

"What?" Korent asked.

Tashan looked at the wall in surprise. Pahmi had kept her voice too low to be heard, or so she thought. Part of her still wanted to be angry with him, but the thrill of hope pushed her on. "This!" She started to push the note through the crack, but remembered just in time that Korent didn't know who she was. She pulled the note back, tightening her hand around it. "I mean, one of the new guards gave me a message. He's from Innsbrooke, and he's going to help us escape!"

Korent paused a moment. "Which one?" He sounded kind of excited, but kind of cautious, too.

"The scary-looking guy. Rishi."

"The one who said you two should be killed?" His voice had an edge now.

"I imagine he was trying to make them think he was fully on their side," Pahmi offered, sitting next to Tashan at the hole.

"What if he's lying?"

"Why would he?" Pahmi asked.

"Because... um..." Korent was silent for a moment. "To mess with us?"

Pahmi smiled and smoothed Tashan's hair. "We'll find out at midnight, I think."

"So he's just going to come and chat with us at midnight? Won't the other guards notice?" Korent asked.

"He said we should pretend to be asleep," Tashan said.

"I imagine he has some plan to make sure it looks natural enough." Pahmi was still smiling. "Thank Maker he came."

"Why you? Out of all the people down here, why does he want to talk to you?" Korent asked.

Pahmi's smile froze.

Tashan looked down, thinking fast. "Maybe because I'm just a kid, and he feels bad for me."

"I'm sure we'll find out more when he talks to her tonight," Pahmi said. "We'll tell you what he said in the morning. I'm sure he has his reasons."

"We'll see." Korent still sounded unsure, but definitely curious.

If the day had seemed to pass slowly before, it was even worse as Tashan paced the cell, counted stones in the walls, ran her fingers across the bars, and waited impatiently for night to come. Pahmi told her to sit down more than once, but eventually sitting would become too boring to handle. Tashan ended up sitting next to the bars, trying to guess what people in the other cells were doing by sound alone.

When it was finally time to lie down, she helped combine the rest of the straw into Pahmi's mattress and dropped onto her side next to the older woman, both of them with their heads toward the bars. She twiddled with the edge of the burlap as she waited. The guards had already changed, but none of their voices sounded like Rishi's. What if he didn't come? Her fingers tightened. That would be the worst. He was her only hope of escape. He had to come.

Tashan was startled by Pahmi shifting positions on the mattress and realized that she'd fallen asleep. She wiggled her shoulders, one of them already stiff, and did her best to look like she was sleeping while finding a balance on the edge of the mattress that forced her to stay awake or roll off. How long had she been sleeping? Had Rishi already come? She stole a peek at the bars, but didn't see a note or any other sign that he'd been there.

Then she heard someone muttering a little ways down the hallway. She strained and recognized Rishi's voice. Relieved, she held still, doing her best to follow his directions.

But his voice didn't get any closer. It just kept muttering.

She took another peek at the bars, more carefully this time, but still couldn't see anything. What was he doing? She wanted to shout to him, to call him over, but managed to bite her tongue in time to stop it from following the impulse.

His voice came a bit closer, but remained a distance away, never stopping the stream of mumbles. A bar rattled, just a little, and Tashan realized that Rishi was doing something with the bars of the cell on the other side of Korent. The muttering occasionally got loud enough that she could make out a few words, mostly gripes about other guards being lazy and leaving him to do all the work.

Her foot jiggled with impatient, excited energy. Why didn't he just come over already? It took a minute before she realized that he was probably putting on a show for the other guards to make it look like he was just checking the cells. If he came and stood by her cell for a long time to talk, it would look weird. But if he was checking all the cells, then him standing by hers wouldn't be so strange.

Still, it would be nice if he hurried up.

It was all she could do to keep quiet as he worked his way across Korent's cell, the sounds of him tapping the various bars more distinct now, as well as his continuous grumbles. Tashan's fingers twitched against the floor beside the mattress against her best attempts to keep still. If this took much longer, she was going to scream.

Finally, Rishi's feet shuffled past Korent's cell and came to a stop outside hers. She almost looked up, but remembered to pretend to sleep. She focused on trying to keep her breathing slow, like a sleeping person.

"Child," Rishi whispered, almost too quiet to hear, "move your finger if you're awake."

Her hand rested on the cold stone floor to keep herself balanced. She slowly wiggled one finger.

"Good. I work with the guards, not in uniform, but I help watch things that happen in the city." His voice rose and dropped just like the same mutters he'd been making before, only a little quieter this time. Anyone else probably thought he was still muttering the same stuff he had been. "I've been following this group for a while to figure out their plans. I never realized they had captured you, or I would have come with far more than just myself. As it is, I'm in a position to gather more information to report back to Innsbrooke as well as sabotage their work from within. Like I said in my note, that makes it hard for me to help much without them finding out who I am—and who you are. Do you understand?"

She wiggled her finger again.

"I need to ask you some questions. Some might be hard, and some you might not know. It's okay." He paused, his fingers tapping on the bars. "Wiggle one finger for yes, two for no, and don't move if you don't know. Have you heard them say who they plan to kill?"

She felt the sick feeling in her stomach as she wiggled one finger.

"Okay. I didn't want to spring it on you if you didn't already know. Have you heard how they plan to do it?"

Two fingers. Then she paused; she had heard something they said about the secret escape tunnel out of the palace. She wiggled one finger.

"Uh..." Rishi tapped more bars. "No and yes. You know a little something?"

One finger.

"Okay. Is it about how they're going to get to your parents?"

One finger.

"Is it at the secret house?"

The place her family were supposed to be hidden during the procession of the guards. Two fingers.

"Are they using the boats?"

Two fingers.

"Do they know about the secret tunnel?"

One finger.

"I see. Do you know more?"

Two fingers.

"I don't have much longer before this will become suspicious. I'll try to find other ways for us to communicate. Watch for more notes." He paused. "I heard you tried to escape once before."

She sighed and wiggled one finger, feeling a new wash of shame.

"And that you do magic, but it's not very controlled."

The shame deepened. One finger.

"You've been trying to master fire first, right?"

One finger. That was how magic worked, by learning fire first and then using that skill to learn others if possible.

"Are you open to trying something different?"

She did look up this time, frowning at him in surprise.

He studiously ignored her, but one of his hands quickly flicked in a gesture for her to stay down and still. As she reluctantly obeyed, he continued. "I'm hiding a note in the crack by the fourth bar up on this side. It has some instructions for you to work on tomorrow. I'll come when I can, and I'll work on figuring out what our options are. Keep your head down and stay safe." With that, he moved on to the next cell, his mutterings going back to the complaints from before.

Tashan started to jump up to get the note, but Pahmi held her down. "We'll get it in the morning. If we move too quickly and another guard sees, they may realize what's happening."

Frustrated, Tashan rested her head on the mattress once more. She wanted to see what the note said. It didn't make a lot of sense—there was no other way to learn magic. Fire was the easiest one to learn, so everyone had to start there. Some people never learned more than that, and others found they could learn other things, but it always had to start with the basics of control. What else was there?

She gave up on that puzzle and let her mind wander through exciting scenes of Rishi finding some amazing way to get them free and her using magic to blast their way out of the dungeon, Korent and Pahmi at her side. She had a smile on her face when she finally fell asleep.

Chapter 5

Tashan woke when Pahmi sat up the next morning. She stretched and rubbed her sore shoulder before remembering what had happened the night before. The note! Tashan jumped to her feet so fast, one caught on the burlap, and she landed face-first on the floor with a grunt.

"What was that?" Korent called.

"Are you okay?" Pahmi asked, helping her up and brushing her off.

"I'm fine." She rushed to the crack and dug out the note.

"Back here." Pahmi steered her to the back corner of the cell, near the hole to Korent's cell. "Keep your back to the doors. I don't want anyone walking past to see that you have this."

"Okay." Tashan scurried to sit next to the wall and unfolded the note so fast, she almost tore it.

"What's it say?" Korent asked through the hole.

Tashan frowned at the writing as if she could better make sense of what it said, reading it slowly out loud.

Follow the steps below. Focus not on your energy, but on what you want it to do. Take your time on each step, and try it more than once before moving on. When you find the right one, stop there and wait for more directions. I've made arrangements to guarantee we'll have a chance to speak by this afternoon at the latest.

First, try to make the air move in your cell like a gust of wind is blowing through. Second, try to make the water in your water bucket swish. Third, try to make the straw under your mattress move. Fourth, try to make the stones in the wall budge.

"Does that make sense to you?" Pahmi asked, looking earnestly at Tashan's face.

Tashan shook her head. "I don't understand. I—"

She broke off and ducked her head when she heard footsteps approaching. Pahmi leaned back against the wall as if she was resting. Tashan chanced a peek when the feet were close enough. One of the guards, the Elf that talked about killing them, glared in at her and Pahmi, then looked at the cell opposite them as he passed. Just a guard on patrol. Tashan took a deep breath and tried to relax.

Once he was gone, she sat up straight again. "I'm not sure what he thinks this will do. Everyone knows magic has to start with fire."

"Are you going to try anyway?" Pahmi asked.

Tashan shrugged. "I guess. It's better than sitting here and doing nothing."

"Very well. Just be careful." Pahmi sat back, then paused and eyed the hole beside them. "What are your thoughts, Korent? You've been quiet."

He had been quiet, unusually so. Tashan moved closer to the hole. "I'm sorry I got upset at you yesterday when you didn't want to help us make a new plan. It's okay. I'm not upset anymore."

He remained quiet a moment longer before finally speaking in a low voice. "Ree, who are your parents?"

Tashan looked at Pahmi, eyes wide. "What?"

"I stayed awake last night so I could listen to what the guy was saying to you. He was too quiet at first, but I managed to hear some of it. I know he said something about these people wanting to hurt your parents. Who are they?"

Tashan kept looking at Pahmi, her chest tight. They weren't supposed to let other people know who she was; they had agreed on that. But they could trust Korent. Couldn't they?

Pahmi seemed to be thinking, then she leaned closer to the hole. "You have to keep it an absolute secret."

"Done. Nary a word shall pass my lips."

"You must keep calling her Ree and not show her any special treatment."

"Ooo-kay." He drew out the word as almost a question, but then continued. "Her name is Ree, and she gets no special treatment. Got it."

Pahmi looked at Tashan one more time, then brought her voice even lower. "Her parents are the king and queen."

There was a long silence. "This is a joke, right?"

"No," Tashan shook her head. "My real name is Tashan. I'm the princess."

"But—but wouldn't you have guards to keep you safe from things like this? How could they capture you and not know who you are? How…" A note of horror crept into his voice. "I refused to help the princess find a way to escape. I—" He sucked in a breath. "I got the princess hurt. By the third moon, I'm such a coward! I can't believe—"

"Shh!" Tashan hissed as his voice grew in pitch and volume.

"Hush." Pahmi's voice came out soft but commanding. "They must never, ever know. Do you understand? They'll kill her if they find out."

His finger emerged through the hole, pointing upward, then bending low downward. A bow. "I swear, I will do whatever it takes to keep you safe and get you free of this place."

Tashan pressed her fingertip against his. "Thank you. I want you to get free, too. I want everyone here to get free."

"Then I'll do it," Korent agreed, withdrawing his finger so he could look through the hole. His face looked a little better today, but not by much. "I'll do whatever it takes to make that happen."

"Regardless of what Ree may wish, the key is getting her out safely," Pahmi reminded them both. "I only hope our new friend really does have a way to make it work."

Tashan looked down at the note once more. Better get started on her part of it. "Okay. I'm going to try this."

Pahmi moved back to the other side of the cell, watching with caution in her eyes.

The expression made Tashan feel bad. Pahmi had a good reason to be afraid when Tashan used magic. Determined not to let things get out of control, she faced the corner and focused. She was drawing up her energy when she remembered the instructions said not to do that. That was the strangest part of Rishi's directions, since the energy is how magic works. How could she do magic if she wasn't focusing on getting her energy in place?

She sighed and focused on the idea of the air moving like wind. And, of course, nothing happened. She rolled her eyes and focused on the idea a second time. Still nothing. This was pointless.

Unless he only meant that she should gather her energy and THEN focus on what she wanted to do. That made more sense. She focused inward to draw up her energy, then focused on the thought of the air moving.

A gust of wind all but slammed her into the wall beside her. She landed on her arm with a yelp as Pahmi cried out in alarm.

Tashan quickly cut off the energy, and the air was still once more. "I'm sorry!"

"What happened?" Korent demanded from the hole. "Are you two okay?"

"I'm fine, I'm fine," Pahmi said, smoothing down her now-wild hair. "I was only startled."

"I'm fine, too." Tashan paused. "Shh—someone's coming!"

They stopped talking as the Elf guard reappeared at the bars. He scowled in at them. "What are you lot up to?"

Tashan kept her head down and didn't answer. Pahmi stayed quiet, too.

"I'm watching you two," the guard snarled, glaring at them. "I heard what you tried to do before. Won't work with me on watch, you hear? Don't care what they said. If I see you trying to pull one over me, I'll gut you on the spot."

Tashan felt cold inside. Something in his voice made her believe he really would do that.

"Leave them alone," Korent snapped.

"Same goes for you, boy." The Elf moved out of sight, standing in front of Korent's cell now. Something banged against the bars, making Tashan jump. "Just give me a reason."

A long silence passed before the guard's footsteps finally moved on. Tashan hadn't realized she was holding her breath until it all came out in a whoosh. "Did he hurt you, Korent?"

"Nah. He's a gasbag. All air, no substance." She could hear his smile, and it helped her feel better. "I'll keep him busy if he comes around again. You work on your list."

Tashan unfolded the note and read it again. Rishi said that she should stop when she found the right one. She certainly had made the air move, but it was too big and out of control, just like when she made fire. So that probably wasn't it.

Step two was the water. She sat down next to the water bucket, then glanced at Pahmi and pointed to the opposite corner of the cell. "Maybe you could sit in the other corner."

The elderly Nim looked like she was trying not to smile. "Wise idea. Thank you."

Once Pahmi was settled, Tashan turned her attention to the water. She was supposed to make it swish. She pictured what that would look like, all the water swishing to one side, then gathered her energy and focused it on the bucket.

The water lunged outward with such a rush that the bucket tipped over with a clatter. The water hit the floor and flooded out into the hallway. Tashan winced and scrambled to get the bucket back in place. "Sorry!"

The footsteps returned, followed promptly by the Elf. He scowled at the water on the floor, then at Tashan, who still held the bucket. "What are you trying to pull?"

"I knocked the bucket over. It was an accident," she blurted. It was true enough. She hadn't meant to knock it over.

His eyes narrowed, glaring at her. "An accident, huh?"

"It's true," Pahmi said, crouching at Tashan's side with a protective arm around the girl's shoulders. "She didn't mean to knock it over."

"Afraid of a little water on your shoes?" Korent called.

The guard turned his scowl toward Korent's cell, then back to Pahmi and Tashan. "The three of you are up to something. I know it."

"Nope. Just me." Korent's tone carried a proud grin.

The Elf scoffed. "Likely."

"What could we possibly do with nothing in our cells and such strong rocks and bars keeping us in?" Pahmi asked.

It was clear the guard was trying to think of an answer to her question. Finally, he shook his head. "I'm staying right here and watching you." He moved back to lean against a section of wall opposite them.

"Could we please have more water?" Pahmi asked.

"No. You can slurp it off the floor for all I care."

Tashan scooted to lean against the back of the cell, watching the Elf. True to his word, his gaze went back and forth between Korent's cell and theirs.

Pahmi settled down next to her. "What do you think?"

"I could try the next one, I guess." She didn't want to risk opening the note again in case the guard saw it, but she remembered that the next one was something about making straw move.

"Are you sure..." Pahmi hesitated. "Will you be able to keep it small enough that he won't notice?"

Tashan's cheeks warmed, but the older woman was right. Her attempts at magic were always too big. The guard would see it and tell Angle-Man, and Angle-Man would know she was practicing magic. Maybe he would take her and lock her up somewhere else so she was alone. Or worse, kill her. Or the Elf might just kill her anyway, like he said. She shivered and hugged her knees.

A hissing noise came from the hole. Tashan glanced over and saw Korent peeking through. She edged closer to the side wall.

"Hey," the guard snapped. "I don't want you talking."

"How could we talk through a solid wall?" Korent asked innocently.

"Just move back and keep your mouth shut." The Elf glared in Korent's direction, then at Tashan.

Tashan slid back to Pahmi's side. How could they do anything with the guard glaring down at them? Rishi said he was finding out their options, but she needed to be working on her magic.

She rested her chin on her knees and stared at the wet floor. Not that it had done much good so far. Maybe this was better. She should just let Rishi come up with a plan and get them out. She only got them hurt or in trouble when she tried to do magic.

More footsteps approached. "Why aren't you at your post?" a guard with a big voice demanded, his face as gruff as his tone.

"These three need an extra eye," the Elf responded, returning the man's glare. "They're plotting something."

The new guard looked over Pahmi and Tashan huddled at the back of their cell, then leaned over to look at Korent. "These three? What makes you think that?"

"They shouted, and then they knocked their water over," the Elf said. He paused. "And they were talking. It was all very suspicious."

The guard stared. "Shouting. Spilled water. And talking. You think that's suspicious?"

"It was how they did it. They did it... suspiciously."

"Go back to your post."

The Elf planted his fists on his hips. "I'm telling you, they're up to something!"

"And I'm telling you to go back to your post." The guard waved a metal amulet of sorts in front of the Elf's eyes. "I'm the captain of this shift, so you have to listen to me."

"A little piece of shiny metal doesn't make you a leader, and it doesn't give you the authority to boss me around," the Elf challenged.

"You'll do as I say, or I'll have you locked up with them!"

"I'd like to see you try!"

The guard grabbed the Elf's arm. The Elf broke free and punched the other guard in the face. Clattering feet came from either end of the hallway, and the scuffle moved out of Tashan's view as more guards joined in. She craned her neck, curious to see if the Elf or the other guy would end up winning.

Pahmi nudged her. "This might be the best chance you get to try the next one."

Tashan shook her head. "It isn't working. I'm just causing more trouble."

"I don't know much about magic, but if Rishi believes you can do it, then so can I," Pahmi said.

"You can't give up," Korent chimed in through the hole. "We have to get you out of here, and if your magic can help, then that's what needs to happen." His eye appeared at the hole, peering through at her. "You can do it."

Tashan glanced at the hallway. Pahmi was right; the guards were so busy with the fight, they probably wouldn't have even noticed if she set off another fireball. This was the best time to try it if she was going to try at all.

"Okay," she finally said. Move the straw. She gathered her energy and thought as hard as she could, *only a little, just move a little, only a little bit!* With that, she focused on the straw in Pahmi's mattress.

The burlap promptly deflated as all the straw shot out across the room. Tashan groaned and buried her face in her knees. She was right. She couldn't do this.

"It's okay, sweetie. You didn't hurt anything. They're still fighting. You can still try the last one if you hurry," Pahmi coaxed.

Tashan shook her head. The last one was making the rocks in the wall wiggle. She'd bring the entire castle down on their heads and kill everyone. "I can't."

"You can," Korent pressed.

"And what if I knock the whole wall down? Or more?"

Neither of them answered.

Tashan buried her face again. She couldn't do anything right, not even a little bit of magic to help save herself and her parents.

"Do the floor," Korent said.

"What?"

He stuck his finger through the hole and gestured downward with the fingertip. "You can't do magic on what you can't see, right? That's why you had to look in my cell to make the fireball before, isn't it? Turn around so you can only see a little bit of the floor. The tiles are stone, just like the walls, so it should be the same. Then if you do make it move too much, it still wouldn't be enough to cause too much damage."

Tashan stared at the hole as his finger was replaced by his eye. That was crazy, wasn't it? Or would it work?

"He's right. And you might not get another chance." Pahmi moved closer to the bars to eye the fight. She gestured for Tashan to hurry.

Tashan looked down at the floor. He was right that the tiles were stone, and if the point was to try to move stone...

"You can do it," Korent repeated, and she heard complete belief in his words. He wasn't just saying it to help her feel better. He was sure she would succeed.

She turned herself around to face the opposite corner, where she could only see a small area of the floor. Pahmi would be safe on the other side of the cell, or at least Tashan hoped so. And it sounded right that the floor tiles moving wouldn't hurt the structure of the castle. She hoped.

She had to focus. There wasn't a lot of time. She looked down at the section of floor and pictured the stone tiles wiggling, then turned her attention inward to gather her energy.

A flicker of movement yanked her attention back to the floor. Had a skitternit run across the tiles? She searched, but saw no signs of the pest. She must have imagined it.

More shouts and running footsteps flew down the hallway. It wouldn't be much longer before the fight was either won or broken up. She had to focus. She looked down at the floor. She had to make the tiles wiggle.

The tiles wiggled.

Tashan yelped and was on her feet before she realized she was moving.

"What happened?" Korent demanded. "Are you hurt?"

Tashan wasn't sure how to answer. That wasn't possible. She must have imagined it. She hadn't even gathered her energy, and magic is done through the energy, so she couldn't have been the one to make the tiles move. And no one else was here to move them, so she must have just wanted it so bad, she thought she saw it. All she had done was think about them moving.

There was an easy way to test if it had just been her imagination. She would just think about them moving again. Scrunching her face up, she looked down at the same tiles and cautiously, carefully, imagined them wiggling.

The tiles wiggled again.

She jumped back a few steps with a squeak, heart racing.

"Ree! What is it? What's wrong?" Korent pressed.

"I did it." She didn't entirely believe the half-whispered words herself. She said them again, stronger now. "I did it!"

Korent peered around as much of the cell as he could see. "I didn't see them moving."

"Because they only wiggled. Like I wanted." The excitement overtook the disbelief, and she jumped up and down while spinning in a circle. "I did it! I made them move!"

"Shh!" Pahmi cautioned, and Tashan realized the chaos outside had quieted down. Someone was talking. Pahmi hurried over and pulled Tashan to sit against the back wall again. "Keep your head down."

Tashan hugged her knees to her chest and rested her forehead against them once more, this time to hide a grin instead of shame. This was impossible, but somehow, it had happened. Without even gathering her energy, she had managed to do magic. She did magic!

"Get him out of here," the big voice said. Apparently the second guard had won the fight. His footsteps paused by their cell. "Boy lost his head, thinking these ones were up to something."

"Do you think they might be?" Rishi's voice.

Tashan's heart sped up even faster. She couldn't wait to tell him about her success.

"Nah. Look at 'em. They couldn't plot their way out of a barn. They mighta tried something the other night, but that was all they got in 'em, and they know it."

Rishi laughed along with the other guard, then paused. "You've got a nasty gash there. Get it looked after. I'll cover the patrol."

"Yeah?"

"Yeah." Rishi's voice lowered. "Sneak a drink while you're there. You earned it. That Elf was a dirty fighter."

"You're telling me." The other guard snorted. "A'right. Keep the place from falling down." His footsteps faded down the hallway.

Tashan chanced a peek and saw Rishi standing where the Elf had been monitoring them. He didn't look her way, so she rested her head again, turning it to the side so she could see him and wait for any signal that he was ready to talk. She hoped that wouldn't take long. The good news would vibrate its way right out of her at any moment.

She felt about to burst when Rishi finally crossed the hallway and leaned against the end of wall separating their cell from Korent's. He spoke low. "We don't have long before things settle back to normal. Were you able to follow my directions?"

"It worked!" Tashan squeaked out. She slapped a hand over her mouth and crossed to sit at the side wall, closer to him. She had to work hard to keep her voice quiet. "I made the rocks wiggle. I didn't even use my energy. How is that possible? Magic is done through energy, right? And rocks are the hardest ones to learn. How come I could do rocks, but not fire?"

"Because that's not how magic works. Everyone's been taught that one type is easier than the others, but actually, each person has their own type that comes most naturally to them. The focus on gathering and forcing energy results in too much being used at once, which rarely works well. Instead, you have to focus on what you want to see happen and let your energy take its natural course to make that happen."

She shook her head. It was hard to understand when she'd been told all her life that learning fire was the only way to learn magic. But the rocks had wiggled when she wanted them to. She couldn't deny that. "So what does that mean?"

"It's a show of Maker's favor that you happen to have skill with rocks. As powerful as you are, with a little training and creative application, you could have every cell in this place open in moments."

Excitement buzzed in her chest. "I could make the locks open?"

"No. You could make the bars fall right out of the walls."

"Is it better to do a full prison break?" Pahmi asked quietly from where she leaned against the wall beside Tashan. "Or to smuggle her out secretly, so they might not even notice she's gone?"

"They know that the three of us have already tried to escape," Tashan offered. "It wouldn't look suspicious on you if just the three of us got out."

"Or we could use a full prison break as a cover while we get out," Korent suggested.

"With all the new recruits they've brought in, I think a prison break would cause more alert than confusion," Rishi said. "There are too many guards watching for exactly that sort of thing. It's more likely we can sneak the three of you out, or just..."

"Just Ree," Pahmi finished for him.

"I want them to come, too," Tashan said.

Rishi stretched like he was bored. "We'll do what we can. Our best bet will be to open the ceiling above you to get up into the next floor. That's ground level, so you can open the wall from there and walk out. The room above you can be busy, but during the night there's rarely anyone there. I'll have to watch and signal you when it's clear."

"Tonight?" Tashan asked, her heart skipping ahead. She would be free, and she could get back to Innsbrooke and warn her parents before these people could hurt them.

"Tomorrow night, I'm afraid."

Her heart tripped flat. "But that's the night before the procession. That's when they're going to..."

"Two problems with tonight. I'm on patrol outside, so I won't be able to signal you. And do you think you'll be able to open a hole in the ceiling and wall without bringing the entire castle down?"

Tashan looked down. She didn't even know how she'd managed to make the floor tiles wiggle, much less how to open up a wall. "No."

"If there was any other way... But there isn't. We'll work on improving your skill, and I'll do what I can to make sure no one sees what's going on when we move."

"But you have warned Innsbrooke of the plot at hand, yes?" Pahmi asked.

Of course. Rishi would have already warned her parents. Tashan felt a little better at that.

"They're aware something is in the works. I've been unable to get any clear messages to them as of yet. I'm doing what I can."

Tashan closed her eyes and felt a sniffle coming. It felt like every time she thought there was hope, it crashed and shattered within moments.

Pahmi squeezed her shoulder. "I'm sure you'll be able to get your message out before it's too late. And we'll work on whatever we need to do to be ready."

"I'll deliver another note later with more instructions." Voices raised from the other end of the hall, and Rishi straightened. "Be careful not to draw too much attention, but try to get more tiles to wiggle. Try to get specific ones. Maybe more than one, and ones that aren't next to each other."

Tashan nodded as Rishi strode away to greet the approaching guards.

"Well, let's get to work," Korent said.

"You mean I need to get to work." Tashan made a face.

"No, we all have hard work to do. You have the hard work of wiggling floor tiles. Pahmi and I have the hard work of cheering you on." He cleared his throat, then said in a dramatic, deep voice, "Yay, Ree! You can do it!" His voice changed back to normal. "How was that?"

She couldn't help but giggle as she stood. "You're silly."

"It's what I do."

Tashan went back to her corner and looked down at the stone tiles, then pictured them wiggling. They responded instantly. It still felt so weird, like it wasn't even her doing it. She didn't know how it worked to do magic without gathering her energy, the way she'd been taught. But apparently it worked, and it definitely worked better than anything she'd tried before.

She wiggled the tiles until she was used to the bizarre movement at so little effort from her, to the point that she started feeling bored with it. Then she focused on only one tile. It moved in response to her mental direction, only it, not any of the others. Pleased, she did it again. Curiosity tempted her. If she could make it wiggle without gathering her energy, what would happen if she did put a little energy into it? She focused on it, then drew up energy.

Before she'd even gathered all her energy, the tile flew upward into the air, almost smashing into the ceiling. She gasped and jumped backwards. "Look out!" But she'd broken the connection to it, and the tile dropped back to the floor and shattered.

Pahmi caught her shoulder and pulled her back a step. "Are you hurt? What happened?"

"What's going on?" Korent peered through the hole.

"It's fine." Tashan's cheeks burned. She'd messed up this magic, too.

"What's going on here?" a guard demanded, storming over to glare into their cell.

Tashan looked down at the floor, where the tile lay in pieces over a conspicuously empty space where it once sat.

The guard followed her gaze, then smirked. "Think you're going to tunnel your way out through a solid rock foundation? Go ahead. I'd love to see you try."

"What's this about?" It was the guard with the big voice, the one who fought the Elf.

"These two think they can tunnel under the castle," the first guard snorted, gesturing to the broken tile.

"No, we don't," Tashan started, but Pahmi gripped her shoulder hard, and she closed her mouth instead.

Big-Voice eyed them, then the tile, then them again. He turned. "Go back to your station. We won't waste time on these two." As the two guards walked away, Tashan heard them talking, but couldn't tell what they said.

"Be careful," Pahmi said, relaxing her grip and giving the spot a gentle rub. "Sometimes it's better to stay quiet and let them come to their own conclusions. And it's a lot easier to remember than a lie." She smiled. "Now, why don't you try it again, but do it like you did before, where it only moved a little?"

"Yeah." Tashan made a face as she returned to the corner. She poked the broken pieces back toward the hole. What if she just made them fly too fast again? If she kept making so much noise, maybe Big Voice would decide they were up to something for sure and would have people watching them all the time.

The broken pieces clacked against each other. She eyed them. Maybe those would be easier to control. They were smaller, after all. She focused on the thought of them wiggling, and they promptly wiggled in response. Scrunching up her face, she focused on the hole they'd come from and the image of them moving across the floor to the hole. They only wiggled in place at first, but then slowly began to shimmy their way toward the hole.

A grin broke across Tashan's face. It was working! She thought for a moment, then pictured the broken pieces coming back together into a complete tile again inside the hole where it had been before. Again, they only wiggled at first, but then pulled themselves closer and closer together. Too slowly. Should she try to put energy into it? No, that was what made them break in the first place. She crinkled her forehead and stretched her head toward them, as if the intensity of her focus and thinking would make them go into place.

The pieces seemed to vibrate in place, then snapped together. She gasped as they neatly sank into the hole, leaving nothing behind but a bit of gritty dust that had escaped when the tile first broke. "I—" She cut her cheer off before she could tell the others what she'd done. The guards might still be too close. She looked over her shoulder and saw Pahmi looking her way, so she pointed to the tile and grinned.

Pahmi took a look, and her eyebrows crept up her sloping forehead. "Good work. Keep going like that, and we won't have any trouble getting out of here."

Tashan felt warm inside as Pahmi patted her back and returned to the other end of the cell. It had seemed impossible, even silly, but now she was starting to believe this might really work. She returned her attention to the tiles, looking at one of the unbroken ones now. She'd made the one tile fly up in the air—too far, but still flying. Could she do it again and control it this time?

Her grin spread. Only one way to find out.

Chapter 6

By the time Pahmi signaled her that the guards were coming to deliver the evening meal, Tashan had made two tiles switch places and was working on getting three to move at once. It was hard to sit still and wait, but she did her best. It became even harder when Rishi appeared, tossing bread into the cells; she wanted so much to tell him what she'd accomplished.

When the guards had finally passed, she jumped to her feet and danced around the cell, though she remembered to keep her voice low. "It's working! We're going to get free!"

Pahmi handed her one of the rolls, smiling. "I think this one's for you."

Tashan turned it over to find the cut edge, then dug out Rishi's newest note. It had a list of tasks, including some she'd already done, like making stones move across the floor or through the air. The rest were things like removing the mortar between two stones in the wall, making stones in the wall move out of place and back in, and moving more and more at a time.

"You have a new assignment?" Korent asked.

Tashan read over the list again, feeling like the sun had left the sky. Pulling stones out of the wall seemed a lot different from rearranging tiles on the floor. And if she messed up with that, she could collapse a wall on top of her or Pahmi or Korent. She'd thought she was doing so well, but this seemed too far above her. "I don't know if I can do this." She hated the words as she spoke them. So much to learn, and all before tomorrow night? She didn't think it was possible.

"I do." His statement was calm and direct, like he was saying water was wet or snow was cold.

"I believe you can," Pahmi added.

Tashan took a deep breath. "I'll try." She bit into the nasty roll and set to work focusing on mortar.

Pahmi had to pull her to bed when it grew too late to continue. "You don't want guards coming through and wondering why a little girl is still up so late, do you? Besides, you're going to need your rest. I don't think we'll get much tomorrow night."

Tashan reluctantly dropped onto the mattress. She'd managed to remove mortar between some of the stones in the wall, but very little else. She wanted to stay up and keep working on it, but Pahmi was right. They needed their sleep, and they needed to avoid making the guards pay any more attention to them than they already did.

Her dreams were a jumbled mess. She arrived at the palace to warn her parents, only to have Rishi block her way in, telling her she had to practice making rocks move before she could go inside. Big Voice and Angle-Man ignored her cries for help as the Elf guard chased her through blurry hallways. Korent and Pahmi sat together on a huge rock that Tashan had to move, but couldn't without crushing them.

Tashan startled awake when a roll smacked into her head. The Elf guard glared at her from the one eye that wasn't swollen shut, then resumed his trudge down the hallway to deliver breakfast. She sat up and picked up the roll.

Pahmi rolled over with a wince and rubbed at her neck. "Morning already?"

"You can go back to sleep if you want," Tashan offered, handing the older woman one of the other rolls.

"No, but it will take a little while to get these old bones upright again." Pahmi waved off Tashan's offered hand to help. "Best to let it take the extra time and adjust. You go on with what you're doing. I'll be fine."

Tashan bit into her roll and looked down at the tiles beneath them. She still didn't feel ready to move stones out of the wall. Her imagination kept showing her pictures of the ceiling caving in and crushing them all. It felt silly after spending so much time yesterday moving the tiles around, but that wasn't nearly as dangerous. And she still didn't really understand it, either. Gathering her energy felt like she was really doing something, even if it did always end up being too much. This way felt like she wasn't actually doing anything at all.

"You ready for this?" Korent asked through the hole, which was now much larger after Tashan had removed most of the mortar last night.

Tashan glanced at Pahmi, then went and sat down next to the hole. "I don't know," she said, keeping her voice small.

"You aren't ready to leave this cell? I suppose it's nice enough, in a way; you could put up some bright curtains or something, but—"

"No," she interrupted, giving him a look. "I want to get out, but I don't know if I can do it. I know you said you think I can, but I don't want to get anyone hurt."

"You won't."

"You don't know that."

Neither of them spoke for a moment, then Tashan spoke again. "Your face looks better today."

"Yeah?" He lightly explored the bruises.

"Less puffy."

He grinned. "See? We're already better than we were before. As for the magic, I've been watching you work on it. I think you're thinking about it too much."

"Huh?"

"I think you're thinking too much. You have to let it do its thing. You just tell it what to do, and the energy is what does it."

She squinted through the hole at him. "You know magic?" She'd heard most Elves didn't like magic.

"I've heard bits and pieces along the way," he said with a shrug. "Will you try something for me?"

She gave him a long look, but at his encouraging nod, she slowly nodded in return. "Okay..."

"Scoot back a pace." She obeyed, and he kept talking as she followed his directions. "Close your eyes. Imagine the wall, exactly how it looks right now. Take another look if you need. Imagine the rocks around this hole. Now pretend you were moving them, and imagine what it looks like for them to slide out of the wall toward you. They're going to float in the air for a moment. Focus really hard on that image. Now pretend you're moving them again, and imagine what it looks like for them to slide back in place."

Pahmi made a strange little sound.

Tashan started to turn to check on her, but Korent stopped her with a louder command. "Keep your focus on the pretending, Ree. Pahmi and I are fine. Do you believe me?"

"Yes," Tashan said, scrinching her eyes to focus all the harder on the pretend wall in her imagination. She still had the rocks partway out of the wall in that image, so she imagined them moving the rest of the way back in place, reforming the hole between their and Korent's cells.

"Do you trust me?"

Funny question. "Yeah."

"Then open your eyes."

Tashan opened her eyes and stared directly into Korent's solid black eyes. She yelped and dropped back in surprise. He sat cross-legged in front of her, grinning.

"What…" She couldn't believe it. He could do magic, too? "How did you do that? How did you get in here? What kind of magic did you use?"

"None." His grin didn't slow down for a moment. "You did."

"Me?" Her voice came out in a squeak. "But I can't… I didn't do any magic, I was just imagining, like you said!"

"I watched it myself." Pahmi squeezed Tashan's shoulder. "Or I saw the last part, that is. I admit, I was startled to watch Korent crawl through the hole you made while the rocks floated between you and the wall."

They were playing a trick on her. It had to be. "But that's not how magic works."

"Do you trust me?" Korent asked again.

It took her a moment longer to answer this time. "Yes. I guess so."

"Then do everything I told you again, but this time, keep your eyes open. Focus on the wall in your imagination, but watch what happens here."

Tashan frowned at the wall. It looked exactly like it had before. There was mortar dust on the ground, but that was because she had removed it last night. *Just do as he says and let them have their joke*, she decided. *Then I can get back to the real work.*

She imagined the wall, which wasn't hard to do with it right in front of her eyes, and once again focused in on the rocks around the hole. Then she imagined the rocks moving out of the wall and floating above the ground.

The rocks around the hole slowly eased out of the wall at the same time she imagined it, hardly making a sound and only creating a light sprinkle of mortar dust to join the rest on the floor. They floated toward her, coming to a stop between her and the wall.

Tashan's eyes widened. "I did that?" She could barely manage more than a whisper.

Korent winked at her. "All you." He promptly climbed back into his own cell through the hole. "I better stay over here, though, or they'll really know something's up."

Tashan couldn't stop staring.

"You... probably want to put the rocks back now," Korent prompted. "Just like you did before. Imagine them going back into place, and keep your focus on the pretending in your head."

She did so and watched in amazement as the rocks slowly shifted back into place. She realized her mouth was hanging open and managed to force it closed. Staring at Korent through the smaller, restored hole, she asked, "I really did that?"

"You really did. I'm proud of you. Also, I told you so. You could too make the rocks move in the walls, and I said so."

She made a face at his smug tone, but she was still too shocked to make any sort of comeback.

Pahmi squeezed her shoulder again, a gentle, happy sort of squeeze. "You did amazing, Ree. I'm proud of you, too."

Tashan unfolded the list. She'd just done one of the hardest things on there, and she'd done it without hardly realizing she was doing it. If she could do that, what else could she do? Part of her was thrilled to find out the answer, and another part was a little bit scared.

But the most important part was that if she could do that, then she could open up holes in the ceiling and walls for the escape. This was really going to work!

Pahmi watched the hallway and Korent gave pointers as Tashan worked her way through the rest of the list. She finished by noon and practiced a few things until she got bored. Then she picked apart bits of straw. She rearranged floor tiles. She tossed little pebbles of grit from the mortar at the wall to see if she could get them through the hole. She played a new style of peekaboo with Korent by making stones move out of the wall and back in at random.

She flopped on the mattress and put her feet up on the wall. "Is it nighttime yet? When is Rishi going to come?"

"We aren't too far off," Pahmi said. "They'll be delivering the nighttime meal soon, and likely our friend will use that as a way to talk to us again."

"I'm bored. And hungry."

Pahmi smiled and mussed Tashan's hair. "You could keep practicing."

Tashan sighed and imagined two of the stones coming to float above her head. They were there within moments. She let them dance around each other for a moment before sending them back. "Done. Now what?"

"I know waiting is difficult. Just keep thinking about what's going to happen once we're free."

Sighing again, Tashan rolled onto her belly and picked at the edge of the burlap, pushing the rough strands to unweave themselves under her fingers. She hated having nothing to do. A yawn pushed its way out, and she blinked hard to push back a sudden sleepiness. She wasn't sure why, but she felt like she'd been awake for days.

Fortunately, the sounds of footsteps and soft thuds announced a guard delivering the food before she was too sleepy to stay awake any longer. Excitement at the thought of communicating with Rishi again helped push the sleepies back all the more, and she hurried to the bars, pressing her face against them as hard as she could, trying to see further down the hall. She couldn't see anything at first, but then the guard came into view. Rishi. She grinned and scooted back to the mattress, trying to think of how she would signal him to tell him about her success. Maybe have a rock come out of the wall and float for him to see? There weren't any other guards right there to see, so it would be safe. She couldn't wait to see the look on his face.

As the moments stretched on, Tashan picked at the burlap more, watching the bars closely even though she could tell exactly where Rishi was from the sound of his footsteps. Why did this have to take so long? He was almost to Korent's cell, but it seemed like he was taking forever.

A sudden flurry of feet on the distant stairs made her sit upright. A big group was coming. Rishi could still deliver a message even if other guards were there, but she might not get her chance to show off. And why was such a big group coming down to the dungeon? Had something happened?

"With us," Angle-Man barked as he approached Korent's cell. As the group came into sight, Rishi fell into step on one side of Angle-Man. Henin was on the other side. The Elf guard who was so sure they were plotting something was barely visible behind Rishi. And they all stopped at the door to Tashan and Pahmi's cell.

Pahmi quickly moved to Tashan's side and put a protective arm around her, watching the guards warily. Tashan held onto Pahmi's arm, feeling better to have the older woman there. Angle-Man had a strange look in his eyes that she didn't like, almost like anger and excitement and greed all rolled into one.

He stared at her hard before speaking. "We just got a message from our men stationed in Innsbrooke. Do you know what it said?"

He seemed to be waiting for a response, so Tashan shook her head no.

"It said that the queen and king have changed their plans. They won't be leaving the palace after all. Which means all of our plans, all of our careful arrangements to ambush them at the escape tunnel, are for naught. There's no point in going to the escape tunnel if they aren't coming out, is there?" He stared again for a moment. "And do you know *why* they've decided not to leave the palace?"

Another pause. Tashan's heart pounded in her chest as she shook her head no.

"Because it seems that our land's beloved little princess is missing. That she went missing on the exact same day that my men caught a sneaky little girl who happens to look like the princess." His eyes seemed to flicker like a fire as his grin spread. "Isn't that something?"

Tashan's insides turned cold as Pahmi's grip on her tightened. They knew. Pahmi said they would kill her if they knew. She looked at Rishi, but his face showed no emotion.

"You really think this little dock rat's the princess?" Henin asked, scratching the back of his meaty head.

"Either she is or she isn't." Angle-Man waved off the question like it wasn't important. "She looks like the princess. That's what matters. Because when we show up at the gates with the missing princess, we'll be escorted directly to the palace for an audience before the grateful king and queen."

Tashan was shaking her head no and wasn't sure when she started. "You can't." The words came out raspy through her throat, which felt like it was closing. She wanted to scream at Rishi to do something, but she knew that wouldn't help.

"They don't take audiences at the palace. They do it at the Meeting Hall," Henin said. "How will that work for preventing reinforcements from getting in?"

"It will be at the palace. We have enough of the guards on our side to help us make sure of it." Angle-Man smirked at Tashan. "I had a feeling she might come in handy."

"Leave her alone!" Korent shouted.

Pahmi pulled Tashan even closer. "I won't let you take her."

"You don't have much choice, old woman. Stand back or face the consequences." Angle-Man gestured to one of the guards, who stepped forward and put the key in the cell door.

Tashan's heart raced as she clung to the Nim woman. The thought that guards were helping these people only added to the shock and horror of the knowledge that they would use her to get to her parents. "No! You can't!"

Korent kicked the wall between their cells, and the weakened mortar gave way. He scrambled through the resulting hole, planting himself between the guards and Tashan. "I said, leave her alone!"

The guards stopped at the open door, startled by the teen who, for all appearances, had just kicked through a solid wall.

Angle-Man's eyes narrowed at Korent. "Stand aside, boy."

"I won't let you hurt her again," Korent said, crouching into a fighting position.

Rishi put a hand on the bars in front of him and tugged lightly at them. "You're not in a position to cause trouble, and we'll have her out of there in moments whether you fight or not. Are you really going to get your face smashed again for this?"

"Yes." Korent's answer came without hesitation.

"Just put him to sleep," Angle-Man said in irritation, gesturing to Henin.

"I have to touch him for that."

"Then touch him."

Rishi tugged at the bars again. "Perhaps he should be restrained first." He glanced at Tashan, then the bars, then returned his focus to Korent. If she hadn't been looking at him at that moment, she would have missed it entirely.

"Then do so," Angle-Man said, shoving one guard forward into the cell and gesturing for others to follow. Rishi and the Elf joined the cautiously circling guards while Henin waited at Angle-Man's side.

Rishi was trying to tell her something. Her breaths came ragged as she frantically thought. The bars, what was he trying to say about the bars? Then she remembered—he had said she could open all the cells here by making the stones move and free the bars. She looked at the place the wall and metal came together, then at him.

He was watching her again, and he gave a tiny nod.

The guards had spread out, forming a half-circle around Korent. Tashan closed her eyes and focused on her thoughts more than she had ever focused before. She'd seen the hallway when she tried to escape, and she drew up that image, holding it tightly as she pictured the bars and the walls around them. She scrinched her eyes, putting everything she had into the image of the rocks around the bars giving way, letting the bars fall free. It felt slower than before, harder, like her mind didn't want to see the imaginary rock change its shape. She pushed all the more, and finally saw the bars drop.

Metal crashes and clangs filled the dungeon. The men still outside the cell hollered as bars came tumbling straight at them. Tashan's limbs felt like wet swaygrass, and only Pahmi's grip on her kept her from collapsing to the floor. She could hear people shouting, the sounds of fighting, Pahmi's frantic breaths as the older woman pulled her to the back corner of the cell, but everything in front of her eyes had become a gray haze. The haze kindly invited her to fall asleep. She thought that sounded like a good idea.

Before she could comply, a hand gripped her shoulder, and she opened her eyes to see Rishi. He was saying something she couldn't make out. A sudden rush of energy shot through her, making her eyes fly open wide. She bolted upright, gasping at the flurry of sound and fighting around her. "What—"

"You have to go now!" Rishi pointed at the ceiling. "Like we talked about. Open this spot here, close the floor behind you, and go out through the wall. Don't let them see you. Don't let them catch you. Go!"

Tashan looked up at the part of the ceiling he'd pointed to. "You're coming too, aren't you?"

"Don't worry about me. Just go," he ordered. He caught Korent's arm mid swing and spun himself with the boy, switching places in a smooth motion.

He shoved Korent back toward Tashan as he dodged a swing from a surprised fellow guard. "Go!"

Korent looked disoriented at his sudden change of position, then his eyes focused on Tashan. "Right. Open it, and we'll boost you up."

This was all wrong. They were supposed to sneak out, and they were all supposed to get away. She didn't want to leave Rishi behind. The bad guys would kill him for helping her.

"You have to hurry," Pahmi said above the din. A guard smacked into the wall beside her. She jumped away from him, but he only sagged to the ground.

There was no choice. Tashan looked up at the ceiling and did the imagining trick. A hole opened up, ready for them to climb through. Korent stood underneath, craning his neck to see and make sure no one was coming to investigate. Satisfied, he beckoned Tashan closer.

The Elf guard grabbed her arm, raising a sword. "Nice try, whelp!"

"Get off her!" Pahmi lunged, grabbing the guard's sword arm and knocking the blade free with a sharp twist. She jabbed an elbow at his face, and his grip on Tashan loosened.

Tashan kicked as hard as she could with a scream, managing to break his grasp just as Korent caught her other arm to pull her away. "Pahmi!" she shouted, reaching for the older woman.

The Elf guard snatched at Tashan's flailing arm, but Pahmi threw her weight into him, knocking both of them to the ground. Panic took over Tashan's mind. She couldn't let him hurt Pahmi!

Korent pulled Tashan under the hole as she flailed, screaming for Pahmi over and over again. "Look at me!" he shouted in her face. She stopped, hiccupping around sobs that she didn't know had come. "This is for your parents. We're all doing it for your parents. We have to go."

The sobs came harder. He was right, but she didn't want him to be right. She didn't struggle as he boosted her through the hole. She turned and reached for him, and he caught her hand, climbing up with her help.

"Oh no, you don't!" The Elf guard jumped and caught Korent's ankle. Korent smashed his leg against the wall, knocking the guard off.

Pahmi reappeared and tackled the guard, but he kept his feet this time, fighting to push her off. The old Nim looked up at them. "Close it!" she shrieked. "Now!"

Tears dripped from Tashan's cheeks. She shut her eyes tight and imagined the hole sealing itself back up. She couldn't bring herself to look to see if it had worked. She already knew it had.

Korent wrapped his arms around her and pulled her tight for a moment, then stepped back and pulled her up to the side wall. "Hurry."

Numbly, Tashan imagined the wall opening up to let them through. The hole that appeared revealed garden hedges on the other side. Shouts rang from outside, some near and high above them, others farther away. The guards were spreading word of the prison break.

Korent pulled her through the hole, and they crouched together behind the hedge. "Close it and stay put. I'm going to check for our best way out."

Tashan held herself tightly and imagined the wall back in order. She'd been so proud of herself when she'd finally figured out how to do magic right, but now it all felt empty. She sniffled and hiccupped, having no more tears left to cry.

Korent reappeared and took her hand. "Stay low, right behind me."

She could hear the guards moving, some of them running inside to help while others watched the outside and made guesses about how the prison break had happened. She heard her name, and she jumped, looking upward, before realizing that the guards were just talking.

Korent put a finger on his lips and pulled her onward. They came to the end of the hedges. There was enough moonlight that she could see they were in a sort of courtyard with a garden, and there was a wall ahead of them which circled the whole castle. This High Lord, whoever he was, really did think of himself as ruler already.

"Can you make one more hole so we can get out?" Korent whispered, pointing to the wall ahead. "Keep it small and low. That's all we'll need. Right there in the shadow of that bush."

Tashan felt like there were weights tied to her body, coaxing her toward sleep, but she forced herself to focus. They had to get out. They had to save her parents. She closed her eyes and created the hole. The ground wobbled a little before she realized she was the one wobbling.

"Just a little further." Korent steadied her with a hand on her shoulder as he looked around, watching the guards for the opportunity for them to run.

Her legs ached from the crouched position before he finally swept an arm around her and dashed across the open space, sliding low into the shadow provided by the moonlight on the bush's wide fronds. He pushed her through the opening, then crawled out after her. "Close it, fast, before anyone sees."

The air between them seemed thick and swooshy, like they were swimming deep underwater. She had to focus hard to get the hole to seal itself back up. It seemed like Korent was talking again. The haze had returned, pushing her eyes closed. She struggled briefly, but finally gave in and fell into a deep sleep.

Chapter 7

Tashan opened her eyes to the sound of wind rubbing creaky branches against each other. It took her a moment to make out what was around her, the moonlight heavily filtered by branches and leaves overhead. She was lying underneath the stretching branches of a bristlak bush, the wide leaves fanned out over her. She realized after another moment that the leaves had been placed there, pulled off the branches and arranged to create the hiding space.

Korent was nowhere to be seen. She peered out between two of the leaves, but saw nobody around. Just more bushes and trees, with large roots jutting up at random from the ground and branches reaching both high and low.

Cautiously, she pushed the leaves aside and crawled out. "Korent?" There was no answer. She turned around a couple times, but nothing looked familiar. Fear pushed her breaths to come faster. Where was Korent? He wouldn't just leave her; she was sure of it. Had the guards found him and captured him again? "Korent!"

Still no answer, only more creaking groans from the tree branches echoing eerily around her. She shivered and started walking, arms wrapped in front of her, eyes searching for any signs of movement. This was all wrong. Rishi and Pahmi and Korent were supposed to be there with her. She couldn't find her way back to Innsbrooke alone. Tears blurred her eyes. She didn't know when she started running, but she couldn't slow down. Korent couldn't be gone, too. He couldn't!

A strong hand grabbed her arm, all but wrenching her to a stop. She screamed and twisted to break free.

"Ree," Korent said, pulling her to face him. "Shh! It's okay, it's just me."

Her legs didn't want to hold her anymore, and she sagged into his chest. "You were gone," she sniffled around weak tears, all her body could manage at the moment. "I thought they found you. I thought I was alone."

"It's okay," he repeated, gently helping her sit. "I'm sorry. I didn't mean for you to wake up all alone." He held out a handful of farberries. "I know that eating helps magic users recover their energy, so I wanted to find you something. I didn't mean to scare you."

She rubbed the tears off her eyes and took the berries, her stomach gurgling at the thought of finally getting something other than the vile rolls. "Thank you." She scarfed them down. Nothing had ever tasted so delicious.

"We're a good distance from the castle now, but we can't rest much." He sounded like he was apologizing. "I don't know how long it'll be before they're out here looking for us. They might be already, so we need to stay quiet and listen for them. Can you help me with that?"

She nodded.

"Good. I think we can be to Innsbrooke by just after sunrise, as long as we keep moving. It's okay if you get tired and need to sleep some more. I can carry you on my back."

Tashan nodded again, but she didn't want him to have to carry her. And he was right, the berries did help her feel stronger again. "I'll be okay." Her stomach gurgled again. The berries had been delicious, but nowhere near enough. "Do you think we could find more berries on the way?"

"We can sure try. Let me know when you're ready to move on."

"I'm ready now." She tried to push herself up and failed. Her fear had made her legs strong enough to move around before, but now they were back to being all worn out.

"We can take a minute to rest. It'll be easier on me, too." He was silent a moment. "I guess I shouldn't call you Ree anymore, huh. Should I call you Princess? Princess Tashan? Her Royal Highnessness?"

A tiny smile pulled at Tashan's mouth. "It's okay to call me Ree if that's easier. Or Tash. That's what my cousin calls me."

"Tash. I like the sound of that."

"Will you come to the palace?"

"I think that's the idea, to go and warn your parents."

She shook her head. "No, I mean after. My mam and da will want to meet you and thank you for all your help."

"I'm not much for ceremonies," he said, leaning back.

"I want you to come. We could have tea. The chefs make really good sweet-glazed hardrolls."

"Well, in that case..." He winked at her. "All right, I'll come."

"Promise?"

"Promise."

She smiled. "Good. And we can have everyone else who helped, too, Rishi and Pahmi..." Unless they'd been killed. Her smile disappeared, and she looked down, hugging her knees to her chest.

"Hey," he said, scooting closer. "It's okay. I'm sure they're fine. Rishi is a strong fighter, remember? He'll make sure Pahmi gets out okay."

"There were so many of the guards." She wanted to find hope but couldn't see it.

"And a lot of prisoners, too. Did you see the looks on the guards' faces when all of the cell bars fell out of the walls? Right on top of most of them, too. You made sure the odds favored our friends."

That part still felt like a blur, but she gave a brave nod. Korent wouldn't lie to her. "Okay. We should go."

He helped her up just as a cracking sound bounced through the space around them. He dropped into a crouch, pulling her down with him, looking around in the dim light. Tashan held her breath, peering into the shadows to try to find who was out there. She didn't see anything. After a long moment, Korent pulled her to move at a crouch. They squat-walked until Tashan's legs ached.

He took another look around, then helped her stand once more. "I think we're clear. We better move fast, though."

Tashan turned around in a circle. She had no idea which direction they should be going.

Korent caught her shoulders and aimed her toward an area with brighter moonlight. "This way." He took her hand and set off at a run.

Her legs were far shorter than his, and it wasn't long before they had to slow down so she could keep up. She gritted her teeth and did her best to run as fast as she could. The sooner they got to Innsbrooke, the sooner she could warn her parents and keep them safe.

They stopped at a tiny stream to drink at one point, then found another berry bush a bit later. Tashan's feet and legs and whole body ached as she plopped down next to the bush and ate one berry after another, swallowing them as fast as she could pick them.

"Slow down," Korent finally said. "Too much of these will make you sick. Come on."

"Okay." She reluctantly tore herself away from the bush and struggled back to her feet. Everything hurt.

"Do you want me to carry you?"

"No, I'm okay." She wanted to keep going on her own as long as she possibly could rather than weigh down Korent. Her feet grew clumsier as they continued on, and it took all the concentration she had to keep from falling on her face.

Finally, Korent slowed to a stop. "Hop on my back."

"I'm okay," she repeated around a yawn.

"We can go much faster if I carry you." He crouched in front of her and waited.

Tashan sighed and climbed on, more of a drag than a hop. Korent adjusted her, then took off at a steady run. She held tight, feeling bad that she couldn't go faster, but he was right—better to do what would get them to Innsbrooke sooner, even if it meant he had to carry her. It didn't take long for the rhythmic bounce of his run to lull her to sleep.

She woke up leaning against a tree with Korent's arm around her. The sky seemed lighter, not quite daybreak, but getting close.

He was asleep, too, but he stirred awake as soon as she moved. "Hey." He blinked hard and stretched his eyes wide to get rid of the rest of the sleepies. "We haven't been resting long. I just needed a little nap."

"It's okay. You won't be able to help if you wear yourself completely out." She looked up at the growing light above them. They really should go, but she didn't want him to be too exhausted. "If you need more sleep..."

"Nope." He bounced to his feet. "A little nap was all I needed." He helped her up, and they took off at a run again.

The sleep had helped a lot, and Tashan found it easier to keep up this time, even though her muscles ached. She kept focused on the goal instead of the pain. Get to Innsbrooke. Warn the guards. Warn Mam and Da. Keep them safe.

She was slowing down again when they stumbled out onto a road carved in the dirt. "Is this... Is this one of the main roads?"

"No, but it is one of the minor ones, I think. It would be the southeast road." Korent grinned. "We're not far now."

Tashan hurried after him along the road in relief. The sun had come up a little while back, and she was starting to worry they wouldn't get there in time. The guard procession would be close to midday. With Maker's favor, they would make it.

Her lungs burned by the time the bridge came into view in the distance. She gasped around the ache and kept pushing herself onward. She could see the guards moving at the end of it, the few who would be keeping watch instead of participating in the procession. They would help her get to the palace and spread the word. She and Korent had made it in time!

As soon as they were close enough, she waved. "Hey! Help!"

The guards moved away from the bridge, craning their necks to see the approaching kids better.

She waved again. "We need help! There are people who are going to try to kill the king and queen!"

One of the guards' eyebrows went up. "It's her!" The two hurried out to meet them.

Tashan let her legs slow down a little as she sucked in air. They recognized her as the princess. They were safe.

But Korent caught her arm and placed himself between her and the guards. "Why aren't you sending for more guards?"

"Stand aside, boy. We need to get the princess safely into the city."

Korent didn't move except to take a couple steps backwards, keeping Tashan behind him. "No, one of you should be going into the city to call more guards and alert everyone to protect the king and queen. Or, at the very least, ringing the emergency bell by the gate to summon more guards. Why didn't you do that?"

The guards looked at each other, then yanked out their weapons and lunged forward.

Tashan gasped as Korent took off into the forest, towing her behind him. She stumbled over roots and rocks, but he didn't slow down. Crashing sounds came from behind as the guards chased after them. The sound was getting closer.

Her legs burned all the more, but she didn't dare slow down or protest. She wouldn't have been able to protest anyway, barely able to gasp in enough air to keep herself going. Her feet were hitting more roots now, her tired legs turning clumsy.

And still the guards were getting closer.

Korent suddenly slid to the side, ducking under a bush. He caught her arms and pulled her to face him. "Run," he panted. "Whatever happens, just keep running."

"What?" she squeaked out around heaving gasps of air.

"I'll hold them off as long as I can, but you have to keep running."

"No!" She clutched his arm. "They'll kill you!"

"They'll kill both of us and your parents if you don't get away. There isn't a choice." She shook her head so hard it hurt her neck, but he caught her face in both hands and made her look at him. "You have to save your parents. You can't let these people succeed. I'll be okay, I promise."

Her fingers tightened. She didn't want to lose any more of her friends. But he was right. And the guards were close enough she could hear the bad words they were saying. She leaned in closer to whisper. "You'll come to the palace as soon as you can, right? After you get away from these bad guys?"

"I will."

"Promise?"

"Promise promise." He squeezed her, then pushed her away. "Run!"

Tashan bolted. Her legs wobbled more by the second, but she clenched her teeth and pushed harder. She heard Korent shout behind her, then the guards shouting. Everything in her wanted to go back and help, to drag him away, to insist they could still escape together. Tears made the trees around her blurry as she kept running instead.

She forced herself to stop thinking about Korent, about Pahmi and Rishi, about how alone she was now, and instead to think about what came next. They had been at the southeast road. She was pretty sure Korent had aimed her west. There was the wide south road out of Innsbrooke, but was it safe? The guards at the southeast bridge had turned out to be bad guys. What if the guards at the south bridge were bad guys, too?

She slowed down, trying to think as she struggled to catch her breath. She couldn't hear the shouts anymore. Had they caught Korent?

Closing her eyes, she took a deep breath. She had to focus on getting to her parents before it was too late. If she didn't go to the south road, she'd have to backtrack to the even bigger east road, the main road through Innsbrooke, or she would have to go to the secret tunnel. But that was where the bad guys would be, right?

No, it wouldn't be. She stopped as she remembered, then sped up again, pushing through scratchy branches and picking her way over the rough ground. Angle-Man said that Mam and Da wouldn't be coming through the secret tunnel after all, so the original plan to catch them there wouldn't work anymore. The way into the palace would be sealed from inside, but Tashan knew a way around that. She would get through the secret tunnel, get inside the palace, find Mam and Da, and everything would be okay.

Her whole body hurt and wanted to stop for a rest, to find something to eat or at least some water, but she didn't dare slow down. They'd already lost so much time. She had to keep going, no matter what.

Her aching, tired body forced her to slow down to a walk at times before she could speed back up to a jog. Moments of fear that she wouldn't get there in time would push her legs to a run, but her body was too tired to keep that pace for long.

Tashan didn't know how many hours had passed before she saw the two big rocks that were shaped kind of like a bird and a tree. She always saw those first when she came out of the secret tunnel. They were backwards, but that was because she was coming from the opposite direction. She sped up, feeling less tired with the eagerness of being so close now. She was going to make it in time!

She passed between the two rocks. As long as she kept going straight, the entrance would be hiding on the other side of those bushes just ahead. She shoved the prickly branches aside, hardly noticing the thorns poking at her arms. She just had to get through the rocky tunnel...

Men surrounded the tunnel entrance. Angle-Man looked up at her from the midst of them, his eyes widening for a moment of surprise before narrowing. "Grab her!"

Tashan screamed and frantically tried to reverse direction, but she tripped over her feet and landed in a heap. She scrambled to get back up, one foot slipping. Hands clamped on her arms and shoulders, yanking her upright to face Angle-Man's wicked grin framed by the tunnel behind him.

She focused past him on the entrance, imagining rocks popping out of the tunnel's walls and slamming into him and the men holding her. Her captors shouted in alarm as the chunks of rock broke free.

One of the hands gripping her tightened, and she felt suddenly weak. The rocks fell to the ground harmlessly. Sleepiness pulled at her eyelids. *Henin!* She clenched her teeth and focused. If he could stop her energy, then she could stop his, too. But how? He was trying to make her sleep again. *Stay awake*, she told herself, focusing as hard as she could on that one thought. *Stay awake. Stay awake!*

Her legs dropped limply, leaving her to sag against the hands holding her while everything turned dark. She'd failed. She hadn't been able to stop him from putting her to sleep. And they were going to take her to the palace and use her to get to Mam and Da. She'd been stupid, charging through the bushes without looking first.

Angle-Man was barking orders as she was lifted into a large pair of arms, probably Henin's. She paused. Why could she still hear them while she was asleep? That didn't make much sense. Was she still awake after all? She tried to move her arms, then her legs, but couldn't. So how could she still know what was going on around her?

It clicked. *My body is asleep, but my mind is still awake.* She'd been kind of successful, at least. But what could she do without being able to see or move?

"Now, let's see..." Angle-Man's voice was suddenly much closer. She felt hands fumbling with the cuff around her wrist, and it fell away. His voice came again with a triumphant laugh as he lifted her arm in the air. "We have her!"

The other voices piled on each other, some in surprise or amazement and others in victory.

Tashan wanted to wrench her arm free, but no amount of struggling convinced her body to move. The grip on her arm released, and Angle-Man's voice moved away.

"Glad you figured out how to stop her this time, *before* she brought the whole tunnel down on us, Henin," a rough voice said as the arms under her shook, as if Henin had been bumped into.

She could hear the scowl in Henin's voice. "I told you, she used to make this big energy draw right before doing anything, so it was easy to tell. I don't know how it's possible, but she's figured out some way to hide it so I don't know she's doing magic until she's already doing it."

"Tell that to the big boss when he finds out you let a little girl stage a prison break," the rough voice grunted.

"Listen up!" Angle-Man barked. "Pilak, rendezvous with the dock group. You're going to stick with Plan C while the rest of us go back to Plan B."

"Wouldn't it be better for all of us to go at once?" Henin asked, his voice making his chest rumble against Tashan's squished arm. "They'll be on higher alert with the princess missing. We might need more swords on our side."

"Our crew will suffice for this plan." Angle-Man sounded irritated at being interrupted, or maybe at being questioned. "Today is our only shot at this. With any luck, Plan B will go smoothly, and we'll be done before anyone realizes what's happening. But should that fail, the queen and king will be taken to evacuate the palace—through the escape tunnel, where Plan C will be ready. Get to it, Pilak. The rest of you, hide your weapons. We won't make it inside if they see too many swords."

"What's Plan B?" a woman's voice hissed nearby.

"Take the princess to the palace and get them to let us in," Rough-Voice responded in the same loud whisper volume.

Tashan's heart beat faster. She couldn't let them do this. She tried again to move, to shout, to do anything, but her body still wouldn't obey. She couldn't even let out the tears that wanted to escape her eyes.

But she didn't need to see to do magic. She'd opened the wall for Korent to climb through while her eyes were closed, after all. She focused on the image of the tunnel, on the rocks that had fallen just inside.

"What the—" Henin roughly adjusted her, his face suddenly too near hers and his musky breath making her stomach turn.

"What is it?" Angle-Man demanded.

"I coulda sworn she was about to do magic," Henin grunted. He shook her, and she felt her head limply wobbling back and forth.

"She's asleep." Angle-Man sounded like the grownups who talked to her like she didn't know anything. "People can't do magic while asleep."

"Yeah..." Henin shook her once more, then settled her back in his arms again. "Guess I was imagining things."

Tashan would have been holding her breath if she could have. She internally relaxed as the men resumed whatever they were working at doing—walking, it felt like now. So she could do magic, but Henin would notice. She didn't want him to know she was still awake, even if it was only kind of awake. If she was going to do any magic, it would have to be strong enough to stop them all at once. She didn't know how long she would be asleep and unable to give a warning to the guards—the real guards—so it would also have to be something that would get a lot of attention at the same time.

She kept thinking through the problem as her body rocked back and forth to Henin's pace. She would be able to hear the wooden sound of the bridge as they crossed it. What if she pulled out the foundation stones to the bridge and made it fall down with the men on it? Could she make that happen before Henin noticed? Probably not. And she would end up falling, too. And guards would come running to rescue them all without knowing these people were going to kill her parents.

Maybe she could create a message on the wall, making words carve themselves into the stone. That would be a good way to warn the guards. But could she finish the message before Henin stopped her? It would have to be a really, really short message. 'Danger'? That wouldn't tell them what the danger was. 'Bad guys'? That wouldn't tell who the bad guys were or what they were doing. 'Assassins'? Maybe that one. The guards might not know who the assassins were, but they would be able to get people to protect the queen and king.

She practiced the writing in her mind, careful not to focus in a way that might alert Henin to her magic. It seemed like not enough time had passed when the sound of the footsteps changed, striking wood instead of dirt path. She did her best to imagine the wall at the south bridge, every little detail she could remember. If she messed this up, Henin might figure out she was awake, and she wouldn't get a second chance.

"'Lo there," a loud voice called from a short distance away.

One of the guards, it had to be. *Please let it be one of the guards.* Tashan focused hard on the image.

"We're going to need an escort," Angle-Man declared. "We've recaptured her. Gather a few of the others."

"Hey!" Henin shook her hard this time, throwing off her focus.

"What's wrong with you?" Angle-Man demanded.

"I swear, she's trying to do magic!"

"Go on," Angle-Man said, his voice turned away as if addressing the guard, then his irritated steps snapped their way across the boards to Henin. A hand roughly grabbed her arm and lifted it above her face, then dropped it. She felt her hand smack her own face on its way back down and internally winced, but of course nothing showed on the outside.

"I'm telling you—" Henin started.

Angle-Man's voice was low and tight. "While I am certain I appreciate your extra caution after what happened in the dungeon, you are placing this whole operation in danger with your constant disruptions. We do not wish to raise any alarms, and you batting her about like that is bound to catch attention. Have I made myself clear?"

Henin was silent for a long moment, then seemed to slump. "Yes."

"Good." The footsteps snap-snapped their way back to their original position.

The image of the wall was still there in Tashan's mind, but she shoved it away. Angle-Man had greeted the guard and talked about 'getting the others.' Like the guards she and Korent had met on the southeast road, these guards here were working with the bad guys. Were all the bridges watched by the bad guys? Hopelessness sank into her chest. She could try to alert somebody, but if they were part of the bad guys, it would do no good. She couldn't move. She couldn't do magic. She couldn't warn anyone.

She was completely helpless.

Tashan hardly noticed as the group started moving again. They apparently encountered only a few curious watchers on their way to the lake's edge, where the carefully guarded dock held boats to get to the palace. She felt a moment's spark of hope—perhaps one of the guards at the dock wouldn't be with the bad guys?—but the friendly greeting between Angle-Man and the guards told her even these ones were in on it. Of course Angle-Man would make sure all the major places they could be stopped would have people on their side standing guard.

They're going to kill Mam and Da, and it's all my fault. The words blared through her mind over and over again. She barely heard Angle-Man telling the guards to sabotage the other boats as Henin's rolling walk turned into a slower dip and rock as he climbed into the wide, flat-bottomed boat. The boats were mainly to transport guards efficiently, and as such held fifty people each. She was pretty sure the group would fill two boats, at least. Too many for the light guard that would be at the palace while the procession was happening. Especially with no Tulvans there to help.

She wished she hadn't bothered trying to stay awake. This was awful, being able to hear what was happening but not able to do anything to stop it. She felt the tears collecting in her eyes again as the boat settled and a steady *swish* told her the oars were moving through the water. She wished she was asleep and didn't have to hear any of it. The bad guys were too good. They had even figured out how to make their plan work if they messed up, since Mam and Da would be taken to escape through the secret tunnel, where the other bad guys were waiting.

A thought slipped into her mind. Unless the bad guys don't reach the palace. Then Mam and Da wouldn't go into the escape tunnel. The guards will only take them if they think the palace isn't safe anymore.

The wooden boat creaked as someone adjusted positions. A light breeze toyed with her hair as she tried to think through what that meant. Part of her didn't want to think about it, but another part of her knew she had to. This was the only way to save Mam and Da and stop these bad people.

She heard a bell ringing somewhere, but her focus was on her thoughts. Henin had already felt her try magic a couple of times, but he'd been yelled at for paying attention. Maybe he would ignore it this time so he didn't get yelled at. Still, best not to take chances. She would have to make it work fast, before he had time to realize what she was doing. And soon. They had to be almost there by now. And big. It would have to be big enough to affect both boats. Maybe she should do it her old way, just to be sure.

The part of her that didn't want to think about it argued that she would die, that she couldn't do this to herself. She silenced it. There was no other way. Mentally bracing herself, she imagined the boats and unleashed her energy into the image of a massive fireball.

Chapter 8

Ari sat just inside the southeast gate, watching the people carefully. Hardly anyone was left on the road; the travelers had already made their way inside the city and found their positions to watch the grand procession. The chaos of the crowds had centered around the major roads, far enough away from this gate that the noise was barely audible.

Her parents were somewhere in that mess, but Ari wasn't interested in the procession. She did the same thing she did every day since hearing Tash was missing: she went to each gate to watch and listen for any news, methodically working her way around the city.

This one was odd today. The guards hadn't even been there when she arrived, and when they did return, they were out of breath and looked like they'd been in a pretty bad fight. And yet neither of them rang the alarm bell or sought help. Guards should never leave their posts, especially not on a big day like today. And they should be calling for someone to at least bring them some bandages and take the report on what had happened. It was like these guards didn't want anyone to know what they'd done.

And so she watched.

Tash wasn't the only one who could sneak around. Ari might not be as good at it as her little cousin, but she could hold her own. She'd been sitting within a couple of paces of one of the guards for a long while now without him noticing anything. She wasn't learning anything, either. There was an occasional strange comment between them, nothing that would help her figure out what was going on and why they were acting weird. She leaned her chin on her hand. Maybe she should move on to the next gate.

Her ears twitched, shaking the messy curls around her face, and she carefully leaned to see the road. A man was running toward the bridge, and he looked no better than the guards.

The two guards came to immediate attention. "What's this about?" the one closer to Ari demanded. "What happened to you?"

"There are…" The man, a particularly thin-faced Nim, slowed his pace but continued forward, panting. "There are people entering the city to assassinate the royal family. They may already be here. We must sound the alarm and get to the palace at once!"

Ari stiffened. The royal family? Including Tash? Was that the reason she'd gone missing?

The two guards looked at each other, then moved forward to meet the man. "Oh, no! Quickly, come with us."

Ari frowned. Why weren't they ringing the bell? Something was definitely wrong.

"The alarm," the man repeated, gesturing to the bell as he reached the bridge. "We have to act fast!"

One of the guards caught the man's arm and twisted it around without warning, forcing the man to his knees. The other one drew his sword.

Panic shot through Ari's system. No time to think. This man knew something about what was going on, and she couldn't let them kill him. She drew up all her energy and didn't bother trying to keep it controlled this time.

The sudden burst of fire in the middle of the bridge knocked all three men flat. Ari bolted out onto the wood, hauled the dazed Nim to his feet, and towed him behind her back into the city. The guards yelled as they struggled to their feet, but she was already dragging the Nim down an alley, out of their sight.

She took a left turn, then a right, and another right, barely pausing before she reached a metal covering half-hidden in the dirt between buildings. Releasing the man's hand, she heaved on the cover. His hands joined her on the edge, lifting it up with a cascade of loose dirt falling off either side.

"Hurry," she said, pointing to the ladder.

He didn't ask any questions, to her relief, and hopped onto the ladder, half-sliding to the bottom. As soon as he was clear, she climbed on and pulled the cover back down behind her. The sunlight disappeared, and she had to blink several times to readjust to the dim light of the underground tunnels.

The man squinted, and she realized it was probably too dark for his Nim eyes to see. She pulled the waiting torch from its holder beside the ladder and pressed it in his hand. "Do you have a way to light this?" she asked. With any hope, he would. She might set him on fire if she tried.

"Yes."

She exhaled in relief as his tinderlight clicked and created the proper spark to ignite the torch. The man's eyes looked creepy and sunken in the low, flickering light. Now that they weren't running, she saw the soot marks on his face and clothes. She cringed at the evidence of her poor control.

He took a brief look around at the stone path they stood on and the wide channel of murky, odious water flowing beside them. "Thank you, miss. You saved my life."

"You said something about the royal family."

"Yes. I have to get to the palace at once." He turned around, clearly disoriented by the multiple tunnel branches on either side of them. "Which way?"

"I'll take you there. You tell me what's going on as we walk."

"Miss, this is no place for someone as young as you. Thank you again, but I need you to tell me which way to go and let me handle this."

Her tongue tried to tie itself up at the thought of standing up to this adult, but she forced it into place. "I said, I'm going with you. Tell me what you know."

He looked up at the cover. "I'm sure they've passed by now. I'll make my own way." He started toward the ladder.

"And I'm coming with you," Ari insisted.

He blew out an impatient exhale. "Can you swing a sword?"

"I practiced with one once."

"Can you control that fireball you made?"

She looked down.

"Then there's no place for you in this. Thank you, but you must stay out of the way of danger. You can help alert the other guards." He started onto the ladder.

Her anger flared at the thought of being left behind with no answers. She caught his arm with her left hand and yanked that sleeve up, letting her gold-toned tattoo shimmer in the torchlight. "Look! I'm Tashan's cousin. If you know anything about where she is or what happened to her, then I'm not leaving your side for a second. I don't care how much you say no. I'm coming with you!" The water behind her splashed as if to emphasize her words.

The man paused, staring first at the water, then at her. "The princess's cousin?"

"Yes." She glared, daring him to try to say no again.

"All right. Come on."

Relieved, she tugged at him again. "This way will be faster."

He talked as she led the way through the tunnels. "My name is Rishi. I'm part of the Innsbrooke guard, in a way. There's a group that wants to kill the royal family—princess included—to get one of the High Lords into power. I'm not sure which one. They were the ones who took Tashan. She escaped last night, and I hope she reached the city. I wasn't able to follow until now."

"So you don't know where she is."

"Not at this moment. But we know the attackers will be going to the palace, possibly through the secret tunnel." He paused. "I don't know if you've heard it, but there's a—"

"Secret tunnel going from the palace into the forest south of the river. I know."

"Right. Either way, we have to get to the palace as fast as we can and get the guards on alert there. And get the guards from the procession." His tone changed to one of regret. "We should have rung the bell on our way past."

He'd been too dazed, and she hadn't even thought of it. She looked down, ashamed. She still had trouble seeing guards as people who would help.

"It's all right," he said quickly. "There's another alarm by the docks. We'll be able to gather the guards. Most likely we'll take the queen and king to the Meeting Hall and set our defenses there while others sweep the city... Though it may be a challenge, working out which guards can be trusted."

She understood that last part completely. "We're almost there." She looked at the tunnel ahead, her chest constricted by all the uncertainties. Tash escaped last night, but Ari hadn't heard any news of the princess being back in the city. Was she lost? Had she been recaptured? Or... worse? She swallowed hard and tried to push that thought away. Tash had to be okay.

She didn't entirely realize she'd sped up her pace until she scrambled onto the ladder and nearly lost her footing.

"Let me go first." Rishi gently moved her aside and started up the ladder.

Ari scowled, but he was probably right. Like he said, she couldn't swing a sword or control her magic. If there were assassins nearby, he'd have a better chance against them than she ever would.

Rishi pushed the cover open just a crack and peered out, twisting and craning to see as far as he could both in front and behind. Finally he was satisfied, and he opened the cover and climbed out, Ari right behind him. They stood in a particularly narrow alley with barely enough space for the metal cover to open between stacks of barrels and crates. This was close enough to the Meeting Hall and city center that the ground was cobblestone instead of plain dirt like in the outskirts. The procession had already begun, from the commotion not too far northeast.

Rishi pushed the cover back in place. "Which way?"

Ari started toward the northern end of the alley, but Rishi caught her and pushed her behind himself. A flare of irritation snapped inside her. She gritted her teeth. Losing her temper wouldn't help anyone right now. This guy knew the bad guys and their plans, so she had to put up with him.

Rishi paused at the end of the alley and checked both directions, then nodded. "I don't see any signs of them nearby. Move fast."

As they hurried toward the docks, Ari caught a glimpse of two boats in the lake, over halfway to the palace. One of the men in the right-hand boat was holding someone small. She squinted, and her heart skipped as she realized it was Tash. "Rishi! Tashan's on that boat!"

He looked, then sped up, waving his arms and shouting to the guards at the docks. "Stop them! Sound the alarm! Those people are assassins!"

The guards charged forward with battle cries that could barely be heard above the din of celebration a distance down the main road from them. None of them went for the alarm bell.

"No!" Ari gasped. These guards were bad guys, too. Her heart raced as she slowed down.

Rishi didn't slow for a moment. He caught the arm of the first guard, used it to deflect a strike from the second, and soon had both of their blades, one in each hand. "Go!" he yelled.

Ari bolted. Everything had turned so chaotic, with cheers and grand music booming and swords clashing and men yelling. She kept all her focus on the bell and ignored the swirling din.

A guard stepped in her path, a Kadrian woman with a pert nose. "Hold it, kid," she barked, reaching to intercept her.

Ari's heart stopped. She wouldn't let her legs do the same. She pushed off into a spin to one side, like in the harvest dance, and slipped past the woman. Fingers brushed against her sleeve without managing to catch hold.

Encouraged, Ari pushed her legs harder. She was so close now. The boats were almost to the two-thirds point. A short wall separating her from the alarm station was just ahead. She had to sound the alarm before they got any further, and all she had to do was jump a little wall.

A hand caught her forearm and yanked backwards. Her feet instinctively thumped and pivoted to keep her from falling over as she yelped in pain, her body forced into a bend by the unforgiving grip.

"Nice try!" The man raised his sword to strike.

It was like everything was too fast and too slow all at once. Tash. The boats. The bell. All the anger she'd forced down came boiling back up in an unexpected rush. "Let go!" she screamed, kicking off the half-wall to drive the full force of a punch into his gut.

The man landed hard with a grunt of pain. He kept his grip on her arm, bringing her to the ground with him.

She screamed and kicked, clawing at his hand until the crippling grasp weakened. Twisting her arm, she squirmed free and bounded to her feet. She jumped over the wall with only the briefest glance around her. Rishi was barely visible in the middle of all the attackers. The boats were three-quarters of the way across.

The guard hollered and lunged at her, but her hand closed around the rope and yanked just as he tackled her. She hit the ground hard under the weight of the man, knocking the air from her lungs. For a moment, all she could hear was her heart pounding in her ears. She regained her breath and heard the sound morph into the alarm bell ringing, the gears turning to keep the large bell crashing back and forth at a rapid pace five more times.

"You little—" The guard raised his sword again.

"Go!" One of the other guards rushed past with hardly a glance their way. "They're coming!"

The man hesitated, then scrambled to his feet and ran after the other guard.

Ari struggled back to her feet. Rishi was already darting down the steps to the docks, looking even worse than he already had. The attackers were all running away. She didn't bother checking behind her to see if the procession had broken and the guards had come running—she was sure they had—and rushed after the Nim.

She reached the dock as Rishi finished untying one of the boats. "I suppose you're going to throw a fit if I tell you to stay on the dock," he said.

"Yup."

"Right. Let's go." He stepped into the boat, then leaped back onto the dock with an exclamation of surprise. The wood at the bottom of the boat seemed to buckle and split, and the craft quickly disappeared into the water.

Rishi stared at the water in disbelief for a moment, then went to the next boat, pushing at the bottom with his foot while keeping his weight on the dock. It did the same. "They sabotaged the boats!"

Ari stared out at the water and the two boats making their way across. So far away. Her heart pounded in her chest. How could they reach her cousin now? Or were they too late already? Tash hadn't been moving. Her hands balled into fists, and tears pricked the corners of her eyes.

Rishi grabbed her by the shoulders. "Listen to me. You can get us to them. You can stop the boats and make it so we and all the guards can get across."

She stared at him, hardly hearing the shouts of oncoming guards responding to the alarm. "What?"

"Your magic. You're powerful, like your cousin, and your talent is with water. You could make this water as firm as solid ground so we can reach those boats."

"You're crazy!" She shook her head. Water was one of the harder elements, and she couldn't even control fire yet.

"Listen!" His tone grew even more urgent. "In the tunnels, when you shouted, you made the water splash. Remember?"

"I didn't do that. It was just a splash!"

"Does that water ever splash like that?"

She blinked. He was right, it didn't.

"You can do this. Focus on the idea of the surface being solid. You have to!"

This was insane. Impossible.

Guards spilled down onto the dock, shouting in a jumbled mess, swords drawn and eyes searching for the unknown enemy.

Rishi pointed to the boats in the lake. "Those are assassins! They have the princess, and they're going to kill the queen and king!" This was followed by an even louder roar and clamor as the guards discovered the rest of the boats had also been sabotaged.

Ari stared at the water, almost ready to jump in and swim after the boats, but there was no way she could reach them in time by swimming. There had to be something she could do. Anything. She couldn't let them—

The air shook as a massive fireball swallowed the right-hand boat and blasted the other boat onto its side.

Ari heard the scream before realizing it came from her. She was running, legs pumping hard, with tiny splashes marking each place her feet hit the water's surface. It was like the water was an ally, a friend eager to help her reach Tash. That was all she could think about. Have to get to Tash. Have to save her.

Heads bobbed in the water as people from the second boat swam to shore. The guards at the palace were moving forward to meet them. Those guards would have heard the alarm, but wouldn't have been able to hear Rishi explain. They wouldn't know these were assassins. Part of Ari wanted to shout out a warning, but her entire being was focused on only one thought. Tash.

Shouts from behind her solved that; strong guards with longer legs than hers had nearly caught up behind her. They need to get to the palace. *Come on, water, help them out, too. Make this reach all the way to shore.* It almost felt like the water responded to her, and the guards passed her as the surface extended itself ahead.

She finally reached the place where chunks of boat still crackled and smoldered. She didn't pause to check around her but dove headfirst off the side of the solidified bridge. The shouts above muted into swirls of fluid around her as she searched, turning one way and another, desperate for a glimpse of her cousin.

Her newfound friend, the water, flowed around her, seeming to help her move through it faster. She could sense something ahead of her before it finally came into sight. Tash, sinking limply toward the bottom of the lake.

Ari's heart pounded in her ears again. Her limbs were turning sluggish. Her lungs and legs ached. She caught Tash's arm and reversed her direction, seeing for the first time that Rishi had followed her into the water. He grabbed Tash around the waist and kicked hard upward, towing Ari along as well. Ari's exhausted body managed to feebly kick along. *Faster. We have to go faster.*

Again, her new friend was eager to assist. The swirling current propelled them upwards to surface. Ari caught the edge of the bridge and pulled herself up, coughing and gasping while Rishi struggled to push Tash onto the surface. Ari grabbed Tash's shoulders and pulled, getting the small girl clear of the water. Her cousin remained limp, and it didn't look like she was breathing.

Ari sucked in air. "Tash?" It came out more like a squeak. Tash couldn't be dead. She just couldn't.

"You can save her," Rishi grunted, still fighting his own way back onto the bridge. "Get the water out of her!"

Ari stared, feeling water, or maybe tears, slip down her cheeks. But Rishi had been right about the water turning solid for her. He had to be right about this, too. She focused on her cousin's chest. *Water, you can't kill her. Get out of there right now!*

She sensed the water in the same way she'd sensed Tash even before seeing her. Ari focused on it hard, repeating her instructions.

The water spilled out of Tash's mouth, and the small girl coughed, her body jerking several times before she was still again. Still unconscious, but breathing. Tash was alive.

Ari pulled Tash into her arms and held tight. The drops falling from her face were unquestionably tears.

Rishi felt Tash's pulse, then gripped Ari's shoulder. "You did good. Hurry, take her back to the dock. The guards will get you and her safely into the Meeting Hall and protect you there."

Ari looked up at the dock. She'd hardly noticed the group of guards there working to keep the mass of curious and worried people in order. She glanced back at the palace. Several bodies lay strewn across the entrance. "Did they..."

"They made it in." Rishi's grim tone matched his face. "There were too many of them. Now hurry. You won't be able to sustain this bridge much longer before you exhaust yourself." He pushed himself to his feet and ran to the palace.

Ari closed her eyes and pulled her cousin tighter. Tash was alive. That was all that mattered. She just had to get the young girl to the Meeting Hall now.

Rishi was right about getting exhausted; Ari already felt like she could lie down right there and sleep for a day. She slowly let out a breath and adjusted her weight so she could stand without losing her grip on Tash.

Tash stirred, and her eyes opened. She stared upwards blankly for a moment. "Ri-Ri?"

The relief flooding Ari brought a smile. "Tash." She pulled the smaller girl into a hug.

"What happened?" Tash drew back after holding tight for a moment. She stared downward. "How are we sitting on the water?"

Ari felt even more drained now. "I did it. I met a guy, Rishi, and he said I'm—"

"You met Rishi? Is he okay?"

"I think so. He went in to help stop the assassins." She put Tash on her feet. "Come on, we have to go to the dock. The guards will protect you there." *And maybe I can get a really long nap.*

Tash tapped at the solidified water with the tip of her shoe. "You did this?"

"Rishi said I can do magic with water." She looked over the span of the bridge. "I guess he was right." Part of her still didn't believe it herself, even with the evidence right under her feet.

"Wait—the assassins?" Tash gripped Ari's arm. "I blew them up, didn't I? With a fireball?"

"You got the one boat you were in. The other one got knocked over, but I think most of them made it to shore. And maybe some from your boat, too." Ari blinked hard to push against the increasingly heavy sleepiness. "Come on, we have to go."

"No!" Tash pulled away and turned toward the palace. "I have to help my Mam and Da!"

"Are you crazy? They'll kill you, too!" Ari caught her cousin's arm before the girl got more than a step. "We have to get you to the Meeting Hall, where you'll be safe."

Tash twisted her arm free and darted out of Ari's reach. "I can't. I can't leave my Mam and Da!"

Ari snatched at her again, but Tash dodged and bolted the wrong way on the bridge, toward the palace.

"Tash!" Ari shouted, but the kid didn't answer. "TASH!"

Chapter 9

Tashan ignored her cousin's shouts, buckling down to run even faster. The doors were wide open, but she rounded the side of the palace instead. Mam and Da would have been taken to the secret tunnel, right where the bad guys wanted them.

She only hoped she could get there in time. There was a safe room before the tunnel, and it was designed to bar from the inside. The door to the tunnel was always kept barred, no matter what. The bad guys would only get in if the guards removed the bar to get Mam and Da out. She just had to get there and warn them before they could open the door.

She reached the grating on the side of the castle that led to the tunnel's air shafts. She stared at the secured bars in dismay. Someone had repaired it since she'd last snuck through there.

Going through the palace would still be way too slow. She focused on the wall around the grate, ready to magic it open, but then realized how tired she felt, like when she and Korent escaped the night before and she couldn't keep herself from falling asleep. She wasn't quite that tired yet, but the fireball had taken up a lot of her energy. It wouldn't be that much more before she wouldn't be able to stay awake anymore.

She'd have to try to pull the grating loose first. She only hoped that whoever repaired it did a shoddy job. She gripped the bars and pulled, then leaned her weight back against it as hard as she could. The top corner budged a tiny bit, then another fraction. She scowled at it and pulled harder. It was moving, but way too slowly.

Stomping feet approached. "I didn't go through all that just for you to run off and get yourself killed," Ari snapped.

Tashan shook her head. "I told you, I'm going to help my mam and da. You can't stop me."

"Yeah, I figured that much out." Ari grabbed the tiny gap Tashan had managed to create at the corner, and leaned back against it with all her might. The grating popped loose, just enough for someone to crawl through. "But I'm not going to let you go off alone and get killed. I'm coming with you."

"Thank you!" Tashan threw her arms around Ari, then spun and ducked into the shaft. "This way!"

Ari took a little longer wriggling through the hole, but caught up soon enough. "Do you have a plan?"

"The bad guys are waiting at the tunnel. They can't get in unless the guards move the bar on the door. I have to get there before then and warn the guards."

"What if they've already opened it?"

She didn't want to think about that possibility. She shook her head hard. "They can't have."

"They might have. You can't just run headfirst in there without being ready."

Tears blurred Tashan's vision. "Then I'll do whatever I can to save them."

Ari didn't answer.

They crawled for a couple minutes before sounds of metal on metal and shouts echoed from ahead. Tashan sucked in a breath, the tears already back in her eyes. They were too late.

Ari tugged at Tashan's ankle. "They're fighting. The assassins are already in there. We have to turn back."

"No!" Tashan swiped a dirty sleeve across her face and tried to crawl forward, but Ari's grip remained firm on her ankle.

"I'm exhausted. You look exhausted, too. And you almost drowned. If we go in there, what good could we possibly do to help? If you go in, you'll only get yourself killed. We have to let the guards do their job."

Tashan shook her head, but she knew she didn't have enough energy left in her to do anything big enough to stop a fight. "I can't."

"You don't have a choice."

She clenched her eyes shut, then turned back toward the sound of fighting. "We can look. Maybe Mam and Da are close enough under the vent that we can help them climb up and crawl out to safety."

"You think your mam and da will fit through here?" Ari's tone made it clear the answer should be no.

"They will if they have to." Tashan hurried forward. The grating on this end of the shaft was still ajar, to her relief. She didn't want to draw attention from the assassins yet, and pounding on the grate would make that a challenge. Pushing the opening a little wider, she crawled out onto the rock. The secret room had been a cave that builders long ago widened and cut. Some of the natural cave structures were still there, like this ledge by the air shaft, the stalactites hanging above them, and the narrow stream of water running along one side of the space.

The usually silent room rang and shook with the sound of the fight. She had to search the mess of people below before she could make out who was where and what was going on. Mam and Da were in the middle, back to back, with Da swinging his sword and Mam using her magic to make the wooden beam that had once sealed the doors fly back and forth, knocking her attackers back. A few guards stood around them, doing their best to fight, but there were too many bad guys trying to get to Mam and Da.

A lot of people lay on the floor, turning her stomach at the sight of so much blood. The doors to the outside were wide open, as were the doors to the palace, and it sounded like more fighting was coming from the palace direction. Probably the other guards who had come across on Ari's bridge.

Her breath caught when she spotted Henin in the fight. "How is he here?"

"Who?" Ari grunted, untangling some of her hair that had caught on the grate as she climbed through.

Tashan pointed and tried to talk quietly while still being heard over the noisy fight. "He's a magic user who made me fall asleep. Except he didn't really the last time because I kept my mind awake, I guess. He was holding me in the boat when I made the fireball. How could he be here?"

"I don't know. You weren't burned up by the fireball, so maybe he was close enough to you that he didn't get burned, either."

Tashan made a face. "I guess. Or maybe he made my magic not work on him. He did that sometimes." She paused. Would Henin know if she tried to do magic to help her Mam and Da now? Would he be able to make it not work like before?

Ari pulled Tashan back toward the small tunnel they had crawled through. "Come on. There's nothing we can do, and if they see us up here, they'll try to kill you, too."

"No!" Tashan yanked free again. There had to be something she could do to help. Another guard fell, and the bad guys moved in closer to Mam and Da. She started to scream for them to watch out, but Ari put a hand over her mouth and pulled her away from the edge.

"They'll hear you," Ari scolded. "You're going to get yourself killed!"

"We have to do something!"

Ari shook her head. "What are we going to do? We might be able to do a little magic, but I don't think I could do enough to make a difference, and I don't think you could, either. Neither of us can use a sword, and even if we could, there are too many down there for us to do much good. There's nothing we can do. We have to get you to safety."

Tashan kept herself planted as Ari tried to pull her by the arm again. Her magic had opened up all of the prison cells in an entire dungeon. If only she hadn't used so much already, she would be strong enough to help. And Ari had made water solid enough for people to walk on. If that hadn't taken so much energy, Ari would be strong enough to help, too.

A thought popped into her mind. When she'd opened up the prison cells, she'd been tired enough to almost fall asleep. Rishi had given her some of his magic energy, and that had woken her up again. If it was possible to transfer energy, then maybe it was also possible to combine energy? Maybe she and Ari had enough left between them to do something.

"Come *on*." Ari pulled harder.

"I have an idea. I need your help."

"Tash, there's nothing we can do."

"But maybe there is, if we do magic together."

Ari stared at her like she was crazy. "What are you talking about?"

"Please, just let me try something? I promise I'll go back out with you if it doesn't work."

Ari looked back at the crooked grate, then sighed and let go of Tashan's arm. "Fine. As long as it's fast and quiet."

Tashan nodded and turned back to the fight. "Hold onto me."

"That's what I was doing," Ari grumbled, resting a hand on Tashan's shoulder.

Ignoring her, Tashan searched the fighters below. It was going to take a lot of concentration to make sure she didn't hit Mam or Da or any of the good guys. And she would have to make it something big and fast so Henin didn't figure out she was doing it and make her energy stop again.

"Okay," she whispered, hoping and praying to Maker with all her might that this would work. She imagined her energy moving, like the stream far beneath them. She guided the current into Ari's hand and let it seek out Ari's energy, then draw it back toward her again. The current settled into a natural loop, from her to Ari and back, over and over again without pause.

It felt like the energy was getting stronger, as Tashan had hoped. Their energy combined. She focused hard on the scene below them, letting images in her mind form the directions for what their shared energy should do. Rocks from the ground burst upward around her parents and the guards. Others dropped out from beneath the bad guys, burying them to their necks. Henin shouted and tried to raise his hands, but he was too late. The crashing sound of metal changed into the grinding sound of rocks moving and attackers shouting in alarm, then outrage, as they found themselves fully imprisoned.

Tashan stared at the trapped fighters, then at her parents in the sheltered circle. They were looking around in fear. They didn't know she was the one who did that. She sent one last direction, and the walls protecting her parents and the guards dropped back down into the floor.

"Wow," Ari said. "Wow."

Tashan looked over her shoulder and grinned at her cousin. Ari looked as energized as she herself felt. Tashan's body had felt worn out and sore, but now it felt like she'd had a day of sleep and another day with the healer. "Yeah. Wow."

Some of the guards stayed by Mam and Da, still looking for a possible threat, while others inspected the prisoners in the floor. Tashan couldn't stop grinning.

Ari scooted forward to crouch on the ledge beside her. "We did it."

"Come on. I want to go down to my Mam and Da." Tashan slid closer to the edge and found the handholds she'd used many times in the past to climb down the wall. A thought occurred to her, and the rock beneath her adjusted itself in response to her thought, turning into a stairway down.

Mam and Da stared in disbelief as she hurried down the steps and ran to throw her arms around them. "Mam! Da! I'm so glad you're okay!"

Henin scowled fiercely as she passed him. "You!"

She felt a wave of sleepiness and shook her head, feeling too giddy to bother with it. "Knock it off!" she ordered him.

He looked stunned and didn't say—or try—anything further.

Mam and Da stared in shock, then pulled her to them and held her tight for a long time. The guards positioned themselves at the door to the palace, but the fighting sounds there were quieting down.

"We were afraid we'd never see you again," Mam whispered, squeezing tighter. "What happened? Did you bring a magic user from the Meeting Hall?"

Tashan shook her head no.

"Then who saved us?"

She looked up at them, feeling warm and happy and safe, but most of all feeling calm and in control like never before. "We did." She looked over her shoulder, but Ari wasn't there. She spotted her cousin still up on the ledge. "Come down, Ri-Ri."

Mam stared at Ari, then at Tashan. "You—the two of you did that?" When Tashan nodded, Mam shook her head. "That's not possible."

"It is. We met a man named Rishi who taught us." Tashan beckoned Ari again, and Ari finally stepped down onto the new staircase and joined them. She didn't cringe as she passed the guards like she usually did, and instead of her normal hesitant look, she held herself upright with something like a challenge flashing in her green eyes.

Mam and Da looked at each other, then back at the two girls. "Then we owe you two our lives," Da said, pulling Tashan close for another hug.

"Yes," Mam said, oddly stiff. She eyed Ari. "What were *you* doing in the palace?"

Tashan stared in surprise. "Mam," she said, raising an eyebrow in disapproval, "she just helped save your life. I couldn't have done it without her."

Ari waved a hand dismissively with a tiny smile. "It's okay, Tash. I need to get back to my parents anyway. I just wanted to make sure you were alive and safe." She eyed Mam with a funny look, but still spoke to Tashan. "I'm confident you're in good hands."

"The best hands for her." Mam's eyes and tone were equally cold.

Tashan looked between Mam and her cousin, perplexed.

Ari started toward the open doors leading outside, but stopped and turned back around, her eyes fierce and fixed on Mam. "For the record, my mam never wanted the throne. She wasn't even interested. You ruined your own sister's life for nothing. We will *never* forget what you did to us." With that, she spun on her heel and marched toward the exit.

Mam gasped. "How dare you speak to me that way? You come back right this instant and apologize!"

"Mam," Tashan started. Mam brushed her aside.

Ari continued forward, ignoring the demands behind her.

"I said, you come back here and apologize!" Mam shouted, waving her hands. The doors slammed shut, and the heavy bar flew back into place, sealing them tight.

"Savini," Da said, a gentle note of caution in his voice.

Ari didn't even slow down. She flicked her hand in an irritated gesture. The stream's flow shot up and smashed into the doors with such force that the beam broke in half. Both doors slammed into the walls behind. One came partway off its hinge, jamming at a funny angle, and the other one creaked loosely back and forth as Ari strode past it.

"You little—" Mam started to thunder.

Da cut her off. "Savini, love. Tashan is back home with us, and we're all safe. Let's focus on that."

Mam still looked furious, but she finally turned back to them. "Of course. I'm sorry." She lightly stroked Tashan's hair. "I let my worry for you get the better of me, and I'm afraid I took it out on your little friend."

Something sounded false in Mam's voice, a sound Tashan had never heard before. Or maybe it had always been there, but she was only hearing it now. She nodded. "I'm sure you'll make it right."

A shocked look crossed Mam's face, but she quickly covered it. "Of course, of course."

"Mam, what was Ari talking about? What did you do?"

"I did nothing wrong." Mam's face tightened, but she put on a calm look that felt as false as her voice. "This is a grown-up matter. It was inappropriate of Ari to be talking about it at all, much less in front of you."

Tashan pressed her lips together, but nodded. "We'll talk about it later. For now, we must find Rishi and go to the forest. He'll take us to the castle where I was held. There are other prisoners, and we have to make sure they're okay."

"We aren't going anywhere," Mam said. "We finally have you back in the palace where you're safe, and—"

"Mam, there are people who helped keep me safe and got me out of there. We can't just leave them."

Mam and Da looked at each other funny again. "My little *paski*," Da said, lightly stroking Tashan's hair as he used the old word for a beloved child. "What happened to you out there? You've changed so much in such a short time."

Tashan started to say that she hadn't changed, but stopped and considered it. She supposed it was possible she seemed different, even though she didn't feel any different. "That may be. But right now, the important thing is helping those people who kept me safe." She turned and hurried toward the palace tunnel.

The fighting was long done now, and guards were busy taking away bad guys and helping their wounded. Tashan heard her parents calling after her, but ignored them as she made her way through the mass of people, searching faces until she spotted him. "Rishi!"

He didn't look good, with blood and bruises all over, but he looked up at her call. He frowned. "How did you get here? I told Ari to take you to the Meeting Hall!"

"I didn't let her." Tashan threw her arms around his middle. "Thank you so much for all your help, Rishi. Can you please take us back to the castle so we can help all the others? And we need to search the forest. Korent had to stop and fight to keep me safe, and I want to make sure he's okay."

Rishi's eyebrows had climbed his sloping forehead as she spoke until they seemed ready to disappear into his hairline. He chuckled. "You don't say."

"I do. Unless you're too injured to help. Is there someone else who knows the way to the castle?"

He still seemed amused, but he put on a serious face. "I'm all right. I'll gather a battalion to go to the castle at once." The seriousness became more genuine. "I'm not certain what we'll find there. The fight didn't go well, and I barely managed to escape."

"Then we must hurry." Tashan started through the crowd again.

Rishi caught her shoulder gently. "Princess, you need to stay here with your parents. You'll be safe here. Let us take care of this."

She frowned at him. "I can't abandon the people who put themselves in danger for me. I won't go into any fighting, but I will do anything I can to help."

He gave her a long look, then pressed his fist against his chest in salute and bowed. "Milady." He proceeded through the crowd at an easy pace to follow, occasionally calling certain guards to come along with them.

By the time they reached the doors leading into the palace itself, Mam and Da had caught up. "Young lady, you will not walk away from us like that," Mam said sharply, catching Tashan's arm. Her face softened abruptly, and she pulled Tashan close. "We were so worried about you, and we're not going to risk losing you again."

Tashan squeezed her mam, then stepped back. "Then come with me. All of these people have suffered, and many helped to make sure I could escape. We have to make certain they're safe."

Da looked at Mam, then back to Tashan. "Do you promise you'll stay right beside us?"

"I promise."

Mam had a funny look on her face. "Very well. But we'll take a second battalion with us."

"One should be enough. We can't leave Innsbrooke defenseless, since some of the guards were helping the assassins," Tashan said. "We have to make sure there are enough good guards here to keep the people safe."

Mam's mouth opened and shut.

Da smiled. "That's good thinking, *paski*. We'll talk to the leaders at the Meeting Hall and make certain there's both enough guards accompanying us and enough remaining here to protect the people."

Tashan nodded, satisfied, and turned to make her way to the exit again. Mam still had a funny look on her face, but she followed along with Da.

When they got to the dock, several boats were just arriving loaded with guards and a few officials from the Meeting Hall with worried looks on their faces. Most of the guards surrounded them and the officials while the rest hurried past them into the palace.

"Princess!" Lord Kizel, an elderly Kadrian with silver hair, clasped her hand. "I'm so glad you're all right. What happened to you?"

"I was captured by the assassins. I'll tell the rest when I can, but right now we must help the other people who were prisoners with me," she said, angling toward the newly repaired boats.

"How awful! Why would they do such a thing?" Lord Mundin asked, a deep frown on his face. He was one of the younger members of the council with dark hair and a wispy beard. "Were you able to hear?"

Tashan started to answer, but paused, looking over the High Lords in front of her. Someone from the council had been behind the whole plot in order to take control of Kenara. Perhaps it would be better to talk about the details only with Mam, Da, and Rishi, to be safe. "I'm afraid I can't discuss it until I've had a chance to talk to Mam and Da about it."

Mundin looked taken aback. "Of course. I only meant that I hope we're able to get to the bottom of it quickly and bring these monsters to justice. I'm grateful you were able to escape and the plot was foiled."

Tashan dipped her head. "Thank you." With that, she resumed her hurry to the boats.

While they were talking, Rishi had organized the guards and apparently consulted with a couple of Pechiks, the highest leaders of the guards, on who should come with them. They loaded into boats and crossed the lake, Tashan using the opportunity to tell her parents about what had happened to her and about the people who had helped her. Once on the other side, Rishi and the Pechiks shouted commands to the guards on the city docks, and soon they were underway.

Tashan rode with her parents on the veelish cart usually used in the guard procession that was supposed to have happened today. They were in the middle of a new procession, this one with a very different goal, as Rishi led the way down the southeast road toward the castle. Since there were only a few guards on the cart with them, the rest riding mounts alongside, before, and behind, Tashan quietly told her parents all she had learned about who was behind the attempt.

"One of the High Lords?" Mam looked shocked, then furious. "Which one?"

"I don't know. I never found out."

"We'll do what we can to discover the culprit," Da said. "Until then, we'll use caution in our dealings with the council."

The trip went much faster with riding mounts on the roads rather than working through the dense forest on foot. Rishi led them off the road for a while, then the castle came into view.

Tashan stood. "That's it!"

The fighters inside the castle stood on guard as the procession neared, many of them filling the top of the wall with bows ready, arrows already resting on the strings. They were going to put up a fight.

Rishi brought his trongial back to ride beside the veelish cart. "Their defenses are strong. We have superior numbers, but it'll take some time before we can break through. Perhaps it would be best for you to move further back while we deal with this."

"Of course," Mam said, nodding toward the driver.

"We have to at least give them a chance to surrender." Tashan looked back at the castle and recognized a few of the guards on top of the wall, including that mean Elf. "Maybe if they know the others are captured, they'll give up rather than fight."

"Yes, we'll try to convince them to surrender first," Rishi promised.

"No, I mean we should do it." Tashan turned to her parents, sure they would agree. They both just stared at her with that same funny look they kept getting. "Their entire plot was to kill us. It'll mean far more for them to hear a call for surrender—and a promise they won't be harmed—directly from us."

Mam opened and shut her mouth. Why did she keep doing that?

Da smiled and gave Tashan another squeeze. "Rishi knows what he's doing, *paski*. He can pass along the message that their plot has failed. And we can wave from back here without any risk."

Tashan grunted in frustration and hopped off the cart. She heard them calling after her as she darted through the ranks. Most of the soldiers were too startled to react. A few made a reach for her, but it was easy to dodge around them or just duck under their hands, since they were mounted so high above her on their stamping trongials.

She reached the front of the battalion and shouted up at the fighters on the wall. "Excuse me. You tried to kill me and my family, but it didn't work. Your comrades and leaders in Innsbrooke have been captured. If you surrender, you have my word you won't come to any harm."

The Elf gave her a furious scowl. "You!" He yanked his arrow back, taking aim at her.

The guards hollered in alarm and rushed forward, but Tashan aimed a hand in the Elf's direction and let her imagination fly free. Before the man could release his grip, the stones beneath his feet dropped backwards. The arrow flew into the air as the man fell, hollering, to the ground below.

The other fighters on the wall shifted and murmured, staring down with fear in their eyes. At the same time, the guards surrounded Tashan. She brushed them off, and they let her, seeing that the threat was gone. They looked almost as stunned as the people up on the wall.

"As I was saying, if you surrender, I promise you won't come to any harm." Tashan studied them. Their fearful shifting gave her an idea, and she made the wall tremble, only slightly. The fighters shouted in alarm, gripping at the stones in front of them in sudden panic. "I hope you understand that I will do whatever it takes to make sure your prisoners are safe and free."

"We surrender!" a pinch-faced Kadrian shouted from the top of the wall, his bow clattering to his feet as he raised his hands. The other fighters slowly followed suit.

Rishi dismounted beside Tashan and shook his head, but Tashan could tell he was impressed. "Nicely handled, Princess. Now please, return to your parents. We'll get—"

"I have to make sure Pahmi and the others are all right." Tashan watched the massive doors in the wall, waiting impatiently for them to open. The fighters above were already communicating the surrender to their comrades, calling orders for the doors to be opened and the prisoners to be brought out.

Rishi chuckled with another slight shake of his head. "Then at least allow me to escort you, milady."

"Very well. Thank you, Rishi."

He thumped a fist to his chest in salute again. "It's my honor."

Tashan started toward the opening doors, but he caught her shoulder, making her wait for some of the guards to go in first. By the time they entered, the prisoners were emerging from inside the castle, blinking and squinting in the sun. Tashan scanned them anxiously. Pahmi had been attacked by that Elf. Had she been hurt too badly?

Then she spotted the elderly Nim in the midst of the group. "Pahmi!" She bolted forward, not giving Rishi the chance to grab her again.

Pahmi looked up, and her eyes lit aglow as she spotted Tashan. "Ree!" She ran to embrace the girl. "You're okay!" they both said at the same time, then laughed.

Tashan studied her friend and cringed at the bruises and cuts she saw. "Come on. I want you to meet my Mam and Da, and we'll get you taken care of. You and all the other prisoners."

Pahmi squeezed her once more. "Thank you, child. I mean, Princess."

Tashan giggled and led the way through the soldiers back toward the veelish cart. "You can call me child. It's okay."

As they neared the wall, she saw the Elf sitting on the ground, watched over by a guard as he rubbed at sore spots from his fall. He glared at her with hateful fury.

She made a half-hearted attempt to resist the impulse, but gave in and stuck her tongue out at him. He scowled all the more as she flounced past, arm in arm with Pahmi.

Chapter 10

Ari pretended to be focused entirely on the snarls in her father's net as she listened to the careful footsteps sneaking up behind her. She waited until Tash had nearly reached her, then spun. "Boo!"

Tash gasped in surprise, then burst out laughing. "How do you always know?"

"Because I'm magic." Ari grinned. That was truer than ever before, as she and Tash learned more and more about their abilities through Rishi's instruction.

Tash stuck her tongue out, then sat down next to Ari and helped her work knots free. "I'm magic, too. I should be able to sneak up on you."

"You'll just have to ask Rishi to teach you to be sneakier." Ari glanced over. "Your parents know you're out again?"

"Not yet." Tash giggled. "They've been acting funny. They say I'm different now."

"My parents say the same thing about me. But I don't feel different." Ari shrugged. "I don't know. You seem a little different to me. Like you're calmer."

"And you seem a little different to me. Like you're funner."

Ari playfully swatted at her cousin, and they both giggled. "Maybe," Ari admitted. "I guess. So, has there been any word from your mystery Elf friend?"

Tash sighed and rested her chin on her fists. "No. Mam says there are a lot of Elf villages in that area, and people travel between them a lot, so if he was hurt, he might have been taken into one of those. She had the guards search the area I lost him, but they didn't find anyone. Mam says that's a good thing, because they would have found his body if he was dead."

"Are you at least going to tell me his name?"

"No." Tash shook her head firmly. "I want to give you a proper introduction when he comes. Da says that we just have to wait, and he'll come as soon as he's able."

"I believe it. No one would turn down an invitation to the palace from the princess herself. Royalty counts for something, you know."

Tash giggled again, then suddenly turned serious.

"What is it?" Ari asked.

"I need to ask you something."

Ari set down the net, worried. She'd never seen Tash so solemn. "Okay."

"What you said to my mam after we saved them..."

"Right." Ari looked down. Tash didn't know about all that stuff, and didn't really need to know. "I'm sorry. I should have thought better before saying that in front of you."

Tash frowned at her. "No, I'm glad you said it. I don't know what it's about, but I think your mam is older, so your mam should have been the queen, shouldn't she?"

"She didn't want to be queen."

"But she would have been if she did want to be, right?"

Ari picked up the net again and tugged at a knot. "Yeah."

"And she didn't just turn it down. My mam did something to your mam. Something to make sure your mam couldn't be queen even if she wanted. Right?"

It took a moment before Ari could answer. "Yeah."

Tash was quiet. "I'm sorry."

Ari shrugged.

"I don't think I could fix it to make your mam queen."

"It's not your problem to fix. Besides, she doesn't want to be."

Tash picked up the net and rejoined Ari in untangling it. "If she had been, then you would be the next queen instead of me. So when I become queen, I'll make you queen instead. It's what's right."

Ari couldn't answer again, feeling tears sting her eyes. She dropped the net and pulled Tash into a tight hug. When she finally could speak, she said, "I don't want to be queen. But I think you're going to be the best ruler Kenara has ever seen, ever."

"You're sure?"

"That you're going to be the best ever? Absolutely."

Tash laughed. "No, that you don't want to be queen."

"Yeah. I'm sure."

"Okay. But if you change your mind, you need to let me know. You should be the next queen, and you can be if you want to be."

They sat together in comfortable silence for a while.

"So..." Ari leaned back in the same way as Tash. "Want to train?"

Tash's eyes lit up. "Yeah!"

Ari slowly stood, brushing off her skirt and making a show of setting the net aside. Then she bolted down the dock. "Last one in the city's a bloated grickle!"

She heard Tash squeal, "Ri-Ri!" behind her, then the sound of small feet thumping after her.

Ari laughed, running faster. She knew she was right. Tash was going to be the best ruler of them all.

THE END

Pronunciation Guide and Glossary

Ari (uh-R*EE) [*the *R* is heavily flipped]

Henin (HEH-n'n)

Ivn (EYE-v'n)

Korent (koh-REHNT)

Lek (LEHK)

Lord Kizel (KEYE-z'l)

Lord Mundin (MUHN-d'n)

Pahmi (PAH-mee)

Pilak (PEYE-lahk)

Princess Tashan (TAW-sh'n)

Ree (REE)

Rishi (REE-shee)

Savini (s'-VEE-nee)

Toshi (TOH-shee)

Yelek (YEH-lehk)

Braybun (BRAY-buhn): A medium-sized nocturnal rodent with long front legs.

Bristlak (BRIHST-laak): A large, bushy plant known for dense branches and succulent leaves.

Da (DAA): The Kadrian term of affection for a father.

Ebrun (EE-bruhn): The western country on Endonsha's landmass, almost entirely inhabited by Hranites.

Elf (EHLF): One of the four races of Kenara, a short people group with large, single color eyes, small noses, and ears featuring a pointed tip.

Endonsha (ehn-DAWN-shuh): A planet with a single landmass covering two-thirds of the surface. This landmass is divided evenly into two countries, Kenara and Ebrun.

Grickle (GRIHK'L): Squatty reptiles with bright tails and a nasty odor.

Innsbrooke (IHNS-br'k): The capital city of Kenara, also the largest city of the land. It is nearly centered beside the wall separating Kenara from Ebrun and has a large lake on the wall side, with two rivers at the north and south end of the city.

Kadrian (KAY-dree-'n): One of the four races of Kenara, a tall people group with high, almost pyramid-shaped pointed ears, flat noses, and wide eyes featuring a vertical slit of a pupil.

Kenara (kehn-AHR-uh): The eastern country on Endonsha's landmass.

Mam (MAAM): The Kadrian term of affection for a mother.

Nim (NIHM): One of the four races of Kenara, a people group with particularly lanky limbs, sloping foreheads, and protruding but curveless noses.

Paski (PAH-skee): An old-language term of endearment for a beloved child.

Raisa (RAY-suh): The Elf honorific for women.

-ro (ROH): The Elf honorific suffix indicating particular respect and honor.

Skitternit (SKIT-'r-niht): Tiny multi-legged insects with long, furry feelers.

Tabe (TAH-bay): The Elf honorific for men.

Trongial (TROHN-jee'l): A vaguely equine mammal with a long, narrow mouth filled with sharp teeth. They are prized as speedy mounts, but must be kept under careful control due to their feral instincts.

Tulvan (TUHL-v'n): One of the four races of Kenara, a people group with small, flat noses, high cheekbones, wide-set feline eyes, and high, pyramid-shaped ears. They have abnormally strong reflexes and agility, as well as retractable claws. They are known for being deeply religious and believe the Maker gave them power so they can serve in defense of others.

Veelish (VEE-l'sh): A lanky equine animal with long, soft fur

Wastik (WAH-stihk): A general Kenaran term for insects or pests which are to be exterminated.

About the Author

I enjoy life with my life-mate and little sprout in the Pacific Northwest. I obtained a degree in Counseling Psychology from Northwest University in Kirkland, WA, which I use to create fully dimensional characters with unique personalities and quirks. In fiction, I'm a huge fan of all things speculative: anything where the rules of reality need not apply. My books include traditional fantasy, space fantasy, post-apocalyptic, and more. When not writing, I can usually be found reading, watching movies, or wasting entirely too much time on the internet. Connect with me at cybishop.com

Read more at www.cybishop.com.